I SEE YOU

Ker Dukey
D.H. Sidebottom

I See You
Copyright © 2015 Ker Dukey Copyright © D.H Sidebottom.

All rights reserved. No part of this book may be reproduced or transmitted in any form without written permission of the Author.

This book is the work of fiction any resemblance to any person alive or dead is purely coincidental. The characters and story are created from the Author's imagination. Any shared files without the author's permission will be subject to prosecution.

Warning: This title contains scenes of extreme depravity; this book is not for the sensitive reader.

Before reading please place a condom over your head because it's about to be fucked.

"Monsters are real, and ghosts are real too. They live inside us, and sometimes, they win."
~ Stephen King

For our Twisted Sisters

Evil is real. It's an entity living under the surface, waiting for the moment when you're weak, when you're beaten down by life to a point that realism blurs and everything we think we know, think we are, differ from reality. That's when you know the monster wears your face, lives your life, and sees through your eyes.

I SEE YOU

Prologue; One

I FOLLOWED THE CRIMSON RIVER flowing down between her pert breasts through the lens; the deep rouge substance slowly travelling over the deep ridges of her breastbone, a pattern developing in the path of blood and leading her life force to pool on the floor around her tiny soft feet, her toes squelching in the puddle.

Click.

Capturing her death was the embodiment of power; watching her dreams leave her so unreservedly and so effortlessly. Witnessing her once strong will desert her and mock her bitterly was rather sad to watch, a void now occupying where fullness had once influenced. If we never had anything to rely on but our commitment to oneself then what had we actually ever had? This girl had been taunted by her mother's condemnations her whole life, and outcast because she didn't surpass her mother's ideals for a daughter. As she swayed before me, her forced splendor now of no support or comfort, then all she had strived for was an irrelevance blown away by the breeze of her final breath.

Click.

Her faint murmured moan brought a smile to my lips, the sound as empowering as seeing the blood now trickle over the small swell of her stomach, her pale skin alive with the adornment of the deep color, her character escaping with each traitorous pump of her heart.

Click.

The heart was such a deceitful thing. She thought she had loved, and had been loved. This small, frail life before me never collected anything but false genuineness all her tragic life. But all she had witnessed was a deception of hope, her mind manipulating every emotion that had been given to her. There was nothing real in emotion. The only genuine thing she would feel was the slowing of her heart and the light fading in her mind. Was it all worth it?

Click.

Her chest stuttered for a moment, encouraging me to click quickly and rapidly, my need to take her final gasp prisoner in the lens a vital necessity. I owed her the idolization of life, her soul fossilized to allow her existence a memory.

Click, click, click.

She gasped, but it was too deep and strong to be the final one. This one was spirited, almost as if she refused to grant me my petition.

Click.

I was growing tired; such a long day. The bitter wind blew through every available cavity in my space, making me shudder angrily, the hairs under my shirt shivering at the chill coming through the window.

Click.

I was surprised, my head tilting and my own eyes widening as hers slowly opened and she managed to focus on me. She frowned faintly, unnerved but surprised by my presence. "W . . . why?" she rasped, her cracked lips splitting and giving my camera more opportunity to work. They never spoke to me. Never. But she was different from them. Personal. I tipped my head, both stunned and humbled by her fight.

Click.

"Why?" she repeated, her voice quiet as her breathing slowed. Lowering the camera, I stared at her. Of course, she wouldn't understand. They never do. Not until the end.

"Because capturing the making of angels, light or dark, is sacred." She didn't scoff or stare at me. Instead, curiously, she nodded faintly.

"You . . . you should know . . ." Her mouth was unmoving as she pushed her vocal chords to do the work for her. " . . . I'm no angel. I have sinned, and as such there is nothing for me after death."

I smiled and stepped towards her. She didn't move back. The chain she hung from still allowed her a little movement. She was simply quite beautiful if her insides were not so ugly. This end for her was a good choice. After all, to her, it was all about appearance. Maybe all this would fill the hole inside her that caused her corruption. I hoped so, for her sake.

"And in the righteousness shall a seraph ripen to become a beast of the heaven." I mocked. There was no faith here, neither her nor my own. There was only life and death and I was here to enjoy hers.

She blinked at my words and as I lifted the lens to finally capture the death that encompassed her, she whispered back, "And in the beast shall an angel of virtuousness flourish. I forgive you."

Two

Devon

Who I am

"WHY?"

Such a simple question, but the answer is unnecessary. For me there is no reason other than I like to watch, capture, and live for a moment in their emotions it's what was normal for me, what was in my blood.

Sin, depravity and murder.

My role behind the lens became an addiction, a necessity. I became a part of their life and sometimes their death, capturing it all in frames.

Click.

Immortalizing them in the most vulnerable, most sacred and soul altering moments of their life. Me and my camera are one, and when I have to step out from behind the eye piece I'm not really sure who I am, or who I want to be. I've always been the photographer, which was my role in our family, albeit a truly dysfunctional one, but we're still a family all the same.

You never really know your family isn't normal until you grow up and realize how incredibly abnormal things were, but by then it's too late, the abnormal is already taking its toll. Not only is it written into your DNA, but it's stamped on your soul and in charge of your actions.

What is normal, anyway?

In our household we had no mother. She died when I was a baby and there was no other extended family that visited. That right there is not normal, right? But how was I supposed to know that? It was just always that way; I have no memory of ever having a mother. There was just me, my big brother, Noah, and our father who worked at the local video store until I was around six years old. After that he stopped going. He never explained why and we knew better than to ask questions. Times didn't get tough. If anything he appeared to be better off, spending more money than usual, spoiling Noah and me with new clothes and toys, especially when he returned from taking one of his weekend trips away. He always left Noah to watch over me on those weekends, and the only adult we would see would be Mrs. Foreman, who worked in the local diner. She checked in on us and delivered supper before returning to her own children. No one really stuck their nose in our business, or didn't care that we got left alone, despite Noah only being around eleven at the time.

No one would have thought he was that young, though. He grew up fast; we both did, and he took his responsibility seriously. That was the only time I actually felt like a child. He played normal games with me; Cops and Robbers, Hide and Seek. That was one of the first things that changed about Noah when our father first began taking him down to the basement, a place I was forbidden from. I missed those weekends with my brother. We never did find out where our father went.

When I was seven years old, my father introduced me to my first camera. He made me take shots of the girls in our street; document them in their innocence while still being in mine so as to not raise suspicions of his perversion to them or their parents. He would pick out young girls in our street or school, and Noah was the one who befriended them. I had the task of taking pictures; that's all it was at first. For a long time I would snap image after image. I was sloppy at first, the camera too heavy and large for my small hands, but I soon became attached to the device, and with a simple click I could encompass happiness, sadness, anger or joy in an instant, to keep frozen in the picture forever. Blonde, brunette, red head, petite, tall, slim build, heavy set; I imprisoned them all in my camera without even knowing why or what my father would do with the images.

One day when I was eight or nine, things changed. Father brought home a girl named Emily. Her name stayed with me; even the sound of her name. I remember the way it breathed through her lips when she spoke it. She had an accent, which made it sound like EM-A-LAY. She was more of a woman to my young eyes, but as I grew and gained knowledge, I know now she must have been around sixteen and a runaway. The girl looked lost. Not in the directional sense, it was the vacant disregard in her large brown eyes that made her a lost soul walking the earth, but already broken by it. I captured her on screen in images and then on film, as I was imparted to do. Her laughing with a careless humor, making her appear younger and more the child she was supposed to be. The lens caught her doing the basic things like eating, but in a ravenous binge, similar to a starving animal being fed scraps. She didn't even chew; just swallowed chunks of a sandwich whole. Her eyes were smudged with worn make up, her cracked lips stained cherry red, leaving an imprint on the rim around the glass she was drinking Dad's liquor from. I followed her around the living room as she began dancing when the chemicals burned in her veins and took hold of her. Her slim body swayed, making her long, untamed hair swirl in her wake. I didn't understand any of this at first, but later, I learned. Her hips moved with experience a girl of her age should never have. I watched her through the lens, learning, feeding from the details it showed me until I was sent to bed and Noah was told to go down into the basement with father and Emily. The basement was off limits at any other time, and when I questioned Noah about what it was he witnessed down there, he told me that was his time, not mine, and warned me not to ask again. The next morning she would be gone, and Noah would sleep in, while I went to school as normal.

There were strict rules in our house, one of which was that we were under no circumstances allowed to talk about what went on inside our four walls. It wasn't until

I was fourteen and my father went away on an unexpected trip that I ventured down into the forbidden basement alone, and decided to watch my work on the TV screen. It was then that I knew what happened down there was more than capturing an image on screen; it was watching emotions come alive in the lens. The camera didn't stop filming when I was sent to my room. There were videos upon videos lined up and labeled. However, the only one I wanted to see after all those years was the one labeled clearly: *Emily.*

I can still remember the twist of nerves from being in the prohibited basement, and as soon as her face filled the TV screen, goose bumps sprung out all over my skin. She was prettier than I remembered; her hazel colored hair flowed in flawed ringlets around a pretty but defeated smile.

Fear is the most powerful display I have ever witnessed in my life, but it wasn't on Emily. As the seconds passed in the top corner of the screen, she was clearly playing a role, toying with the camera and teasing Noah with the sight of her naked flesh. But it was Noah's fourteen-year-old eyes that held the fear as my father's voice commanded him to fuck her and wrap his hand around her throat.

"Be the aggressor or the victim, Noah," his deep, unmistakable voice warned.

When Emily realized Noah's hands were a little too tight around her neck and this wasn't just role-play anymore, fear flashed briefly in them. Her arms flayed and fought off Noah but he was broad and strong. It wasn't long before a tear slid from her eye; acceptance of her fate.

Noah's tears dripped from his green eyes, falling on to her face like a signature of his sorrow, his sin. Any soul he once had poured from him until nothing good remained. This was what changed him; this was what shaped him into the cruel, twisted man he is today. His sobs as he squeezed became growls, his arms locking as his hands choked the life from her, their naked bodies still joined.

I never spoke to Noah about what I saw because his trips to that basement were almost as regular an occurrence as our father's. Different girls came, and like the others, went. I documented each one, and in some small way they became a part of me. Their spirit never really dies if they live on the screen or in the image I create of them, right?

When I was sixteen everything changed. Father introduced us to a woman he married a few months later. Trudy Vallis, mother of our new stepsister, fifteen-year-old Courtney. The first girl I ever loved. She was so dainty; auburn hair, and eyes that were a perfect mix of blue and green. Tiny features decorated porcelain skin and a huge personality exploded from every pore. She became my best friend. She showed me life outside of my father's habits and rules. She made me feel normal.

I wasn't normal though, and neither was the family her mother married into. When the first fight between her mom and my father turned physical, Courtney hid in my closet with her hands over her ears. She bit into her lip so hard her teeth punctured the flesh and blood stained her pink blouse. The next day at breakfast, with her mom sporting a black eye, she was back to her infectious self like nothing had happened, making me realize maybe we weren't the only non-normal family out there. Courtney had been around violence before.

Trudy and father's toxic relationship gained too much momentum on the night before Noah's twenty-first birthday. It wasn't just toxic between those two; Noah never really took to Trudy or Courtney, and often would have all-out fights with our Father over them being there and him marrying her. It never made sense to any of us why they married, but I got Courtney from their deranged coupling so I didn't need to have answers. Noah was in the kitchen this particular night when Trudy was drilling him about getting his own place.

Traumatic brain injury occurs when an external force injures the brain.

Her eyes were still open for the hour it took for father to arrive home. Noah's fist connected with her jaw in a moment of anger. Her flaying arms were unable to protect her from hitting her head on the kitchen counter while falling.

Dead, gone forever. The consequence of a focal impact upon the head, a single forceful blow to the cranium, and lights out. They had many arguments but this one had unimaginable consequences for as all, and I sat and watched the emotions transform my father's features, watched as the sin of his and Noah's deeds did nothing but make him growl, "What the hell am I supposed to do when Courtney asks where her mother is?"

I didn't feel shock or grief witnessing first-hand the murder of a human being. If anything, I felt special. What's more powerful than living in the moment of someone's death?

I became so obsessed with documenting every woman who came into the house that my main thought when looking down at my dead stepmother was that I didn't capture it on film. How fucking not normal had I become?

"Let me have Courtney." Noah's words still echo through my mind on repeat every time I go to sleep.

I remember the heat. The flames grew so fast, and the blaze roared and tore through that basement like a tidal wave crashing against the shore, swallowing everything. Courtney was different. She was my friend, my stepsister. I didn't want the basement to claim her. I was numb as the only house I'd ever lived in was smothered in a hellish inferno. Flames whipped out and licked at my surroundings. Eventually neighbors appeared, screaming, "Is there anyone in there?"

I had text Courtney and Noah to meet me at the grocery store. Noah had replied that he was out taking care of business and that Dad had gone to get some supplies to get rid of Trudy, so no one should have been in there but he had lied.

"Oh God, Devon, what have you done?" Noah's shocked face stared at me as the flames lit up behind him, highlighting him like something from a supernatural film.

"You can't have Courtney. She's not going down there," I whispered.

"She was already down there, Devon. They both were. You fucking killed them both."

Running, running in the rain with no shoes on as the fire lit up the night behind me. That's the last thing I remember about that night. I woke up the next day on a bus with Noah. He took care of us and soon found people like us; sick, depraved, not normal. They had needs and a craving Noah was all too happy to feed . . . at a price. There was nothing Noah wouldn't do, and his brutality on women gained him an unhealthy clientele and a reputation that would make us wealthy and lead us to this life. To her life.

Three

Devon

'Look how beautiful she is. Her terror so alive in the image,' I muse, looking at the portrait displayed on the screen. They never see it coming, not one of them accepting their fate. Everyone expects happiness, love, their life to be a fairy tale, yet no one ever believes in the bad things that can happen to them. Maybe fairy tales are a myth for a reason. For some, the story doesn't have a happy ending.

I mark the file as completed then attach the files to the email and type Noah an accompanying message.

I think he will enjoy these; she was truly a great subject.

Marissa Isabel Raye. I will miss her, and it's a shame the contractor didn't want us to document her in the aftermath of his end game. That was always the favorite part for me. But each client was different, and each with his or her own unique desire and cravings. Some are tame and just revenge plots, others are much more sinister. Mr. Clark only wanted us to document her with her new lover, and then in her grief when she was delivered the news of his murder, courtesy of Mr. Clark.

It would have been so much better to capture the murder on film and then show that to her, but Noah is the one who meets with clients and designs their plans; I'm just the one who documents them.

The screen blurs before me. Pushing my chair back, I stand and lift my arms high above my head, stretching my weary muscles.

I spoon extra coffee granules into my cup, then heap in a sugar, pour the water then take a hefty mouthful, wincing at the heat but sighing at the caffeine rush. The week has been busy, the numerous contracts Noah and I have dealt with taking my energy to a low point. I need something to take my attention away from work for a while.

A ping from my laptop alerts me to a new email. My heart leaps in excitement but my mind sighs tiredly. The blood in my veins heats when I fire up the secure email from Noah, and a smile lifts my lips. It's a female. Always the best.

Client—1325

Mark–
Name—Nina Francis Drake
Age—24
Address—126 Lime Ave

Brief -
Rape—vaginal—anal
Personal recorded surveillance.
Pain—high
Record assault.—Yes
    Courtesy call—No.

Roles.
Client—No
Noah—Contact—Rape.
    Devon—No contact—document.

I love it when they want surveillance. It makes it all the more real and personal. Many just give the name, and the brief is either plain assault or murder with no documentation. It excites me when they need the approach, event and outcome. That means I'm useful.

I fill my camera with a new memory stick, sling the strap around my neck then make my way out.

My head tips when the front door finally opens and she steps out of her home. She's pretty. Noah will be pleased.

Click.

Her long blonde hair falls over her shoulders and onto the swell of her large breasts. Her waist is small but her hips are wide, making her soft and real. She has long legs, her pink skirt displaying her pale skin from her thighs downwards. She reminds me of someone but my mind won't let me search for her.

Click.

"Morning, Mr. Ilavich," she shouts to her neighbor who is mowing his lawn. She smiles at him and my heart rate quickens. It's not a reaction I'm accustomed to, but something about her, her innocence maybe, draws me in. Her smile is one of the most stunning things I have ever witnessed through my lens, the edges of her lips touching the apples of her cheeks with the size of her smile. She is simply beautiful.

Click.

"Are you on the late shift again, Nina?" Mr. Ilavich asks.

Nina nods. "Yep, again. Eleven finish."

"Would you like me to feed Ginger?" he asks. I presume with that name it is her cat he's referring to.

Nina shakes her head but smiles. "No, he's good, thank you. Just fed and watered him so he'll sleep now until I'm home."

Click.

I'm captivated by her soft voice; her unique tone has a hint of an accent I can't quite place but it's the way her eyes sparkle naturally that makes her all the more enthralling.

She climbs into her little red car and waves to the gardening man before pulling away.

Click.

Mr. Ilavich winds the wire around the mower as I pull away from the curb and take the same route as Nina, but I keep my distance. I know what I'm doing by now. The last thing I want to do is spook her so soon. It's such a shame

I won't get to actually touch her. For once I'm jealous of Noah. It never bothered me, the physical side to our business. I have always been happy with just photographing and documenting but my fingers itch to trace the contours of her striking cheekbones.

I can't get the vision of her out of my head as I pull into the nightclub parking lot and park at the opposite end to her.

Her door opens and her legs are the first thing I see exiting the little Audi.

Click.

She climbs out then opens the rear door and grabs her bag before disappearing into the club's side door.

Running my tongue over my dry lips, I throw the camera onto the passenger seat and wait.

I've been documenting her schedule for a week, and every new day is like seeing her for the first time. She steals my breath and holds me captive behind the lens. After watching her go into the bar for her shift, I leave. It's dark when I arrive back at Nina's. Her damn cat is blocking the kitchen door when I try and push it open. "Move, Ginger." Like a perfect pet, it meows then walks away, allowing me access to its home.

My eyes scan the place. As suspected, it is pristine, everything clean and in its place. The whitewash cupboards and blue counter make me smile when I see the matching checked tablecloth. She takes pride in her home.

The hallway is long, with two doors leading off it. The first is an under-stairs closet. Her shoes are thrown in haphazardly and for some reason this makes me smile more. She isn't as OCD as I envisioned. The lounge is small but decorated snugly, the deep plum walls making it appear cozy and warm. The single couch lets me know she lives alone, and the lack of photos around the place also states she doesn't have close family.

The third step creaks when I venture up the stairs. I make a note of that. Ginger meows again and curls his soft body around my ankles as I step into her bedroom. My heart stills when a feminine floral scent strokes my senses, her unique fragrance making my dick hard. I close my eyes, fighting back the anger. I never react personally to any of them and I can't understand what is different about this girl, but I refuse to give the desire any power. She is beautiful and I need to get laid, that's all this is. I'll call Simona later and have her suck my dick to take the edge off. She's a 'high class' whore that I use when I need to vent sexually. She values my business-only attitude, which works well for me.

Nina's duvet is floral, but the walls are a soft peach, taking away the girly aspect of the room and making it gentler to the senses. I run my gloved fingers over her hairbrush then pick it up and slide it into my bag. Her perfumes and creams are placed perfectly straight on the vanity, her cosmetics piled into a small basket. Picking the pinkest lipstick, I slip that into my bag. I rearrange her perfume, not enough to incite alarm, just enough to make her pause and question herself.

Sitting on the edge of her bed, I pick up her pillow and bring it to my nose, inhaling her aroma. Damn, she's sweet, her scent almost intoxicating. I inhale again like my life depends on it. Her essence coils deep in my veins, my blood injected with something that makes my whole body shiver.

I growl under my breath. What the hell is it with this woman?

Placing the pillow back I pull in a deep breath then get to work.

Four

Nina

I SWEAR I HAVE A poltergeist. Either that, or Ginger has become so advanced she now has opposable thumbs. I pick up my body lotion from the bed and place it back on the dresser where I could have sworn I left it. I take the few items I grabbed from the store from my bag and collapse on my bed. I hate working long shifts at night. I'm always exhausted but too wired to sleep. I welcome the weight of Ginger as she leaps up onto my stomach and kneads the fabric of my work shirt.

"Don't wreck another one, Ginger. These come out of my pay check." I sit up, balling her into my arms and rubbing my nose against her wet one. "You want some dinner?" I'm sure she's rolling her eyes at me.

As I stand I hear something drop to the floor next to my foot; the nametag from Ginger's collar. I bend down and pick it up. The small metal loop is all bent. *Strange.*

"Looks like you need some new bling." I baby talk her all the way down the stairs, not surprised that she takes the opportunity to dive through the cat flap as soon as I place her on the ground. "Love you too, deserter!" I call after her.

I notice Mr. Ilavich's garden lights on through the window, and a woman's laughter echoes through the night air.

'No way does he have a woman there,' my mind whispers in disbelief.

I race up the stairs, turning off all the lights, and sneak to the window in my spare room at the back of the house. Shadows crawl across the floor when I tilt the blinds, letting the moonlight pour in. I'm stealthy in my nosy neighboring, using the curtain to shield my body from sight.

"Oh my God."

A young woman is naked, sitting opposite Mr. Ilavich in a lawn chair, her legs open and everything on display as she pleasures herself. I can't peel my eyes away even though I desperately want to.

I slide my cell from my pocket and scroll through to the picture that Tricia added to her number. She's photoshopped her face onto Chris Hemsworth's wife's body. No one would believe she's twenty five; she acts like a teenager.

I dial the number and place the cell to my ear while it rings.

"If this is a booty call you have the wrong equipment for me. Sorry, sugar," she says.

"My neighbor is having a booty call, or filming a porno. I'm not quite sure," I reply.

"Eww, she's like . . . ninety!" she shrieks.

"No, not Bernadette. She passed months ago, her house is still vacant. Mr. Ilavich!"

"Oh my God, that's worse," she screams, causing a giggle to bubble out of me. "Tell me what's happening?"

I twitch the curtain to get a better look through the slits in blind. "They're in the back yard, he's fully dressed and seated opposite a blonde woman who can only be my age." I inhale a quick breath when it dawns on me that she's more than my age. She looks just like me, if I were nude and skanky, with Daddy issues. "What else?"

"She's naked and playing with herself."

Another screech shrills down the line. "Argh! Like rubbing her tits or full on finger banging?"

Gross!

"The fingers." I shudder.

I quickly look away and dance around in a circle on my tiptoes when he unzips his pants. The hand not holding my cell is now covering my eyes. "I can't look, I can't look!"

"Take a picture!"

"What? No! Eww!"

"Come on, I need to see it to believe it." She giggles. I sneak back to the window and look out. The woman has moved between his legs and her head is bopping up and down in his lap. I follow his navel, up his chest, neck.

"Oh fuck." Fighting for the pull cable on the blind to close them, and instead opening them, making me scream and panic, I quickly abandon the cable and draw the curtain across and run to my room.

"What the hell is happening?" Tricia calls down the line.

"He was looking up at the window."

"Oh God, that's creepy and wrong. He is so gross."

"Who's finger banging? Nina?" I hear in the background. Tricia's boyfriend, Simon.

I hear slapping sounds and an *oomph*. "Yeah, Simon. Nina is finger banging to me down the phone, dumbass."

"That's a show I'd pay to see." More slapping and then the phone goes dead. Simon's crude remarks aren't new and I grit my teeth, once again annoyed by his childishness. He often makes jokes about me and Tricia getting it on for him. I don't understand why she would stay with a man like him, but who am I to judge? My past is made up of a few douchebags along the way.

After another ten minutes I sneak another peek next door to find the party has moved inside. I'm hoping Mr. Ilavich and his choice of gardening will be a one-time occurrence.

I avoid him for the next week.

Five

Devon

I CREEP ACROSS THE BACK wall like a shadow, watching her as she works. Her interactions are polite and gracious, but she doesn't flirt with customers like the other girls do, hoping for bigger tips. She wears very little make-up, but nothing about her is understated; she's too naturally appealing to pull that off. Her clothing isn't as revealing as the other girls', yet she oozes sex appeal nonetheless. It's the sway of her hips when she glides through the club from table to table. The smile she uses only for the one waitress, Tricia. It's the movement of her body when she relaxes into the music and her body flows in rhythmic sways to the beat. It's those eyes piercing through a darkened, crowded club, like a beacon of purity and light.

Her hand rubs over the back of her neck when she thinks no one is watching her but I'm not the only predator out here in the shadows—I'm just the most dangerous one.

I leave an hour before she does so I can let myself into her house with a key I had made from the spare set she keeps in the plant pot next to her shed. I've been staying in the empty house that backs on to hers so I can document her precisely; every perfect detail of her. She is by far the most fascinating mark to grace my lens, and grace it she does. I capture her giggles when her cat waits for her at the door every time she returns. She takes such comfort in that feline, I almost feel guilty snatching it up by the scruff of its neck and taking it with me. *Guilt?* I roll the word around my mouth. Guilt is an emotion I haven't touched in a long time. I rearrange the magnets on her fridge, take the cat, and leave.

Meow, meow. The fuzz ball keeps wrapping itself around my ankles and looking up at me as I sit by the window, waiting for Nina to come home. Usually cats have an instinct about evil, yet here it is trying to seduce the very worst kind of it. I'm under no illusion I'm a monster. I was born from one, raised by one, and brother to one who lacks any trace of ever owning a soul. I'm a monster, and despite the draw I feel, oddly but so intensely for Nina, I'm still here documenting her so Noah can destroy her. This is the job, how it's always been.

My heart thuds in my chest when her headlights illuminate the side of the house as she pulls onto her drive. She comes to the side of the house where her front door is, and startles when the man next door to her pops his head over the fence.

Mr. Patrick Ilavich, forty-nine years old, wife died ten years ago. He fathered no children and lives alone.

I capture her grimace in an image.

Click.

Watching her close up through my lens, her hair falls around her face, shielding it from him. She turns and offers him a practiced smile, and takes the mail he offers her.

"Ginger?" she calls out, searching her surroundings, and her eyebrows pull together in confusion. Disappearing into her house and returning with a box of kitty nibbles, she shakes the box and calls out for her stupid cat again. "Ginger, where are you girl?" After fifteen minutes of hopelessly hunting for her cat, she goes back inside, and the lights flick off one by one until the house sits in complete darkness.

"Looks like time for some shut eye, Ginger."

Six

NOAH

THE BUSINESS CELL CONSTANTLY RINGING wakes me from the deep void I fall into when I sleep. I've always wondered what it would be like to dream, but all I see when I close my eyes is black. Wrapping my hand around the morning wood tenting the sheets, I think about the woman Devon has on surveillance for a high paying client. He informed me in his email that she's not like any we've marked before, but to me they're all the same. They are all playthings for me to torment. I let my mind wonder into the acts I plan to force on her, and the grip on my cock tightens, my fist pumping over my shaft. Devon said she's blonde and petite; I've always had a thing for blondes, ever since I didn't get to fuck the mouth of our stepsister. Courtney's image comes to mind as I thrust into my fist. Devon had such fondness for that girl; she was his weakness.

It's hard to believe he's from the same bloodline as our father and me; it didn't take much for me to be completely corrupted by the draw of debauchery, but for Devon it took their deaths, and even now he's showing signs of empathy for this new mark, asking for detail on the client. He has never done that before. My balls tightening bring me back to the task at hand. I picture Emily, my first kill, the tears in her eyes, and that brings me over the edge. Ribbons of cum spurt onto the bed. I swipe the sheet up and wipe my cock down. I hate how my memories show me my life. It's like seeing my life in a movie rather than reliving it. My memory has been that way ever since I killed our stepmother. Although I didn't feel anything for her, my mind punishes me for the act and only shows me my memories looking down, as if I'm floating above everyone.

Meh, so I'm a little insane. Who can blame me with the upbringing I had?

The ringing is back on the work cell and if it's the client calling to cancel today's mark I'm going to be pissed. Payment isn't the issue; they pay when we design the plan, and whether they follow through or not, the fee is always non-refundable. I'm not a realtor; they're not buying a fucking house. My service is one of a kind and comes with extreme risks. That's why all my clients come recommended by another; they then become their guarantor. If anything goes wrong by fault of the client then both client and guarantor pay the price. The price being their lives.

My blood feels static in my veins; the sexual release doesn't quash it. I need a release of a different nature. I grab my cell and answer the call.

"You're through to the servicing department," I answer.

"Reference 1320 confirming the go ahead for renovation."

Ah, he's not cancelling. Excellent.

"Renovation will take place within the next two hours."

"Confirming courtesy call needed."

"Noted. You'll receive a courtesy call. Make sure you're in a quiet, private place when receiving."

I end the call and stretch out my muscles.

I open the parcel Devon left for me with everything I'll need for today's mark, and get ready.

It's only a twenty minute drive to the client's apartment. His wife will be in bed sleeping as she works night shifts, and her husband, *my client*, has left for work already. In an hour, her lover, also married, will let himself in and slip into her marital bed and they'll spend the afternoon fucking before her husband returns home. Whore. Today will go a little differently for them both.

I park a few blocks away in one of my many cars used for work, and keep to the shadows of the buildings. It's early so it's deathly quiet, with only a gentle breeze rustling through the leaves of the trees.

I keep my head down and hoodie up as I slip in the front door left open for me by the client. It's dark throughout the apartment with only bands of light penetrating through the blinds. I place my bag on the floor, pull out my overalls, and slip them over my clothes before I venture any further into the house.

I love it when their eyes expand when they first see me standing there like a crime scene investigator. They're shocked and confused, but deep down a part of them knows they're going to die. I gain a piece of their soul before they've even exhaled their last breath.

Her plump, bare legs hook the quilt beneath them. She's a fuller build, wide hips and a big ass. I can see the appeal. I enjoy a woman with meat on her bones; more to play with.

I take out the burner phone and dial the number for the courtesy call. When he picks up the line I mutter, "Refurbishment in progress," and place the cell on the bedside table on speakerphone. Opening my bag back up, I take out the zipped plastic bag with the positive pregnancy test she thought she hid well enough from her husband, along with her lover's watch and hair sample taken from his apartment by Devon. I put on the latex gloves before handling the contents.

I place the test on the floor near her bed. Clenching the wristwatch, I pull until the link breaks. I whistle loud enough to startle her.

"What the . . . ?" She gasps.

"Catch." I throw the watch to her, which she instinctively grabs as it flies towards her face. I tighten my left fist and swing it out at her as she tries to scurry from the bed, entwined in bed sheets. I connect with her jaw, her lip tearing open from my knuckle. She's dazed, her eyes unfocused as she tries to grasp onto reality. She tries to stand so

I jab her nose with another punch, enjoying the popping sound it makes as the connection breaks the bone. Blood showers out, staining the floor and my boots. *Perfect.*

I launch forwards, wrapping my hands around her throat and straddling her as she topples backwards. I make sure to use more pressure with my left hand than my right. She flays beneath me as her hands reach up and grapple at my chest, but it's weak and too late. Her eyes bulge, the blood vessels popping as water pools and drips from the corners. She's gurgling as her lungs scream for air. Blood runs in rivulets from her nose and down her cheeks like a cerise dam burst. Shaking her body with the final squeeze, her arms drop heavily and her mouth falls closed. Her dead eyes look blankly up at me.

I climb from her body, end the call on the cell, and chuck it into the bag. I drop a couple of her lover's hairs on her. I slip off my boots, and make my way to the back of the apartment to wait.

Twenty minutes later, her lover arrives. He enters the back door with no shoes, just like Devon predicted. Apparently lover girl didn't allow shoes on the carpets. I wait for him to pass though the kitchen and then I sneak from the pantry and out the back door, taking my overalls off and taking his boots with me. I make the urgent call to the police about hearing a woman screaming then hurry back to my car. I drive to the underpass where a group of homeless people set up camp, and I take the bag, dropping it in one of the fire pits they have burning.

I pull out the piece of paper, the last remains of evidence from this job, which is a typed note from Devon.

I SEE YOU

Details to remember:

Lover is left-handed.

Make sure to get bloodstains on boots and switch them over, they're identical.

Leave the hairs I took from his comb on the body. He will feel compelled to go to her and touch her, leaving enough evidence and the fingerprints we need, but we have to take the extra measures.

Seven

Nina

"MY TIPS ARE INSANE TONIGHT. I love stag parties," Tricia says, rounding the bar and hip bumping me.

She's right; my tips are the same as my week's wage tonight alone. The groom is a marine, which means a packed house just with their crowd. They are loud and boisterous, but most are respectful and hot as hell. The barmaids have been putting on a show with body shots, but despite the atmosphere, I feel sick with worry.

"Damn, Nee. Who killed your kitty?"

My stomach plummets with her choice of words. I grab her arm. "What? Why would you say that?"

Her eyes widen and she breaks out into hysterics. "Calm down, cat lady. I was kidding. Jeez. I meant you're acting like a sour puss. What's up?"

"Ginger didn't come home last night or this morning. She's never done that before. I'm worried something's happened to her." I twist my mouth and shrug, feeling a little lame for being bent out of shape because my cat abandons me, but she's my family. The only one I have now. My parents were in their late fifties when I came along, somewhat a horrific surprise after they'd planned to never have children. They'd been desperate to get me out of the door since I hit sixteen, so being the good daughter I was, on my eighteenth birthday I packed my meager things in a suitcase and left. They hadn't even realized I'd gone until I phoned them three days later with my new address.

"She's a cat, Nee. She'll be off exploring and shit. You worry too much. Trust me. Put a can of tuna out tonight and watch her come purring."

Maybe Tricia's right. Cats are independent; that's the reason I got a cat and not a dog.

I jump up from my stool. My shift finished ten minutes ago and I'm dying to take a shower.

"So how'd you do in tips?" Tricia asks.

I know I won't be able to leave without telling her; she makes me tell her every night and then bitches me out for earning more than her, even though she doesn't need the money. Tricia is a trust fund baby; her mom actually paid her to leave the family home after she caught her at seventeen, trying to seduce her stepfather. I don't think she ever really felt like she belonged. Her mother is a highly religious, career-minded woman, and her dad was killed in action when she was four, and it left her troubled. Our similar abandonment by our parents and their strong faith is what formed such a firm bond between us.

"You really want to know?"

"Yes, hit me."

I pull out the rolled up bills from my bra and wave them at her. "$656." Her jaw drops. I push my hand into the pocket of my jean shorts and hold up the coin. "And 50 cents."

A beer coaster flies at me from her outstretched hand. "How is that even possible? You don't even have any boob showing!"

I duck from the coaster skimming my head and take off, giggling as I go.

I pull into my drive and exit the car, running to the front door to escape the downpour that has opened upon me. I do a quick sweep with my eyes of the backyard but see no Ginger, which isn't surprising in this weather. A shiver races through my body as I shake off the light dampness and drop my things on the table.

"Ginger?" I call out, but she doesn't come. What if she's been run over and killed, or she's injured and waiting for me to come rescue her?

I go to the fridge to rummage for something to eat. A sigh leaves me when I know I'll be eating an omelet for the third night in a row because I haven't done any grocery shopping again. Slamming the fridge closed, a couple of alphabet magnets drop off and clatter to the floor. Crap! I bend over to retrieve them and my heart pounds in my chest when I place them back on the fridge and notice a cluster of letters separated from the others.

They spell out 'MEOW'.

I involuntarily step backwards, my eyes darting around my house. Am I going crazy? Oh God, if Mr. Ilavich has been in here . . . I dart out the front door, and the rain drenches me in an instant but I don't care as I run up the three steps to his porch and hammer my palm on the door.

"Mr. Ilavich! Mr. Ilavich, are you in there?" The lights are out and his stupid dog isn't barking. I push the letterbox open and call for Ginger through the gap but there's no noise apart from the rain beating down over the house. Tears burn my eyes as my body shivers from the soaked clothes sticking to my body.

I storm back to my house, slamming the door, and as I pick up the phone to declare my cat has been kidnapped, probably by my old, porn performing pervert neighbor, I hear the cat flap open and my wet furry baby saunters in.

"Ginger!" I grab her up and berate her for disappearing on me like that.

After feeding us both, I take all the magnets from the fridge and shove them in a drawer as punishment for my own paranoia. Damn, I let my worry go too far, making me act stupid. I'm glad Mr. Ilavich wasn't in. How embarrassing would that have been? I take a shower and then curl up in bed with Ginger.

A loud persistent banging wakes me from slumber. I grab Ginger, who's sleeping half on my head, half on my pillow, and sit up to listen. The banging continues so I slip out of bed and down the stairs. It's my front door. Someone's there.

"Who is it?" I demand.

"It's me, Nee!" Tricia cries.

I drop Ginger to the floor and unbolt the lock, swinging the door open to find a wringing wet Tricia. "He was cheating on me!" she howls, falling against my body.

My arms wrap around her as the rain from her clothes seeps into mine. I usher her inside, lower her into a chair, and put the kettle on.

She sniffs and wipes her nose across her sleeve. "Five fucking years I gave him and he was screwing that whore Tracy from next door."

Once the kettle finishes boiling, I fill our mugs and take the seat opposite her, carefully placing the cup between her trembling fingers and guiding them back around it until she has a firm hold. "I mean, she's not even fucking pretty and she's fat!" she whines, which turns into a hiccupping sob. "And she's older than me! Fat, old, ugly whore! Thanks a lot, Simon. This will do wonders for my self-esteem."

I reach for her arm and squeeze but I don't say anything about her neighbor Tracy being gorgeous, every single pound of her, or the fact Tricia spreads her legs for anyone who shows her attention. It's Tricia's right to vent and as her best friend I will agree with her that the neighbor's a mess. "Don't let him have that power over you. Most men are pigs. Look at me with Rob. He cheated and lied the whole way through our relationship," I remind her.

"Is that why you turned to pussy?" She laughs through a sniffle.

I roll my eyes at her and pick Ginger up from winding

her body around my legs. "Yes, because this pussy doesn't leave me for another pussy."

"No one would leave you. Rob only took off because you wouldn't believe him when his assistant claimed he cheated. No one would cheat on you, Miss Perfect."

I sip my drink and ignore her snide dig. Truth was, Rob was brilliant, talented, and driven and he could have given me a good life, but the passion on my part just wasn't there. When his slutty assistant made a play for him and claimed he took her up on the offer of sex on the side, I used it as an excuse to end things. Truth was Rob loved me so the chances were she was making it up but men in love can still do stupid things and whether he did or not staying together wasn't fair to either of us.

Eight

Devon

I'M EXHAUSTED. I CAN'T REMEMBER falling asleep, but I'm waking up to the sound of Nina shouting for her cat. I look at the monitors of the cameras I placed in her house while she was at work, and then through my telescope to see her storming from the direction of her neighbor and into her house. I turn my attention to the kitchen camera's live feed. She's soaking wet from the downpour and every inch of fabric is clinging to her body, highlighting her incredible figure. Her hair lays limp, stuck to her face and shoulders, and when I notice her hardened nipples pushing through her t-shirt, my cock stirs to life. What the hell?

I jump up to clear my head, opening the front door so I can get some fresh air. After a couple of minutes I return to the monitor and watch as she paces the floor. She reaches for the phone on the counter but gets distracted by her cat. Fuck! I look around, and sure enough, the little fur ball escaped when I had the door open. The relief and admiration for that stupid animal lightens her eyes. She's so beautiful. How can she be so alone? If a man like me wants to have her smile upon him, her hands to touch his flesh, how can she not have a harem of lovers spoiling her with jewelry and taking payment in just knowing her, feeling her embrace, discovering her inside and out?

The blinking icon on my laptop draws my attention. I have unread mail from two hours ago. *Noah.*

> Case: 1320 Refurbishment complete.
> How did she handle the cat death?

Why does he want the details of her sorrow? She's a job number to him. He's going to ruin all that beautiful, and not once have I ever felt this pang of remorse in my chest before her.

I open a new email and reply.

> Decided against death and went with making her question her own sanity instead.

I know he will like that; he's all about the torment, mentally and physically. I know I won't get a reply from him anytime soon. After a completed job I sometimes won't hear from him for a couple of days. He likes to bask in the memory of his plan.

I grab some food and settle in for the night once I see her asleep in bed with that dumb cat asleep on her head.

Her chest rises and falls in contentment, and oddly, mine does too.

When I awake again it's 3am and her friend from the place she works at is banging down Nina's front door. I watch as Nina rouses and goes down to check it out. They end up chatting about men being assholes and that's my cue to sleep again.

I hear movement from the bathroom monitor and lose my breath as I come around from the burning nightmares that plague my sleeping hours. The sun's up and Nina is completely naked. Her rose colored nipples are peaking to perfection, her smooth skin free from blemishes. She's tidy with herself; there's only a small patch of hair decorating her mound. My eyes travel over the slick, gentle curves of her body, and my own comes alive. I need to stroke the ache building. I release my dick from my trousers and let my hands grasp the end, my thumb massaging the pre-cum there around the tip. She's in the shower but her body is visible through the frosted glass, teasing me with the delights it bears. I thrust my hips into my fist as her hands rub all over her flesh, and I want her hands to be mine. I grunt from the pleasure my dick is feeling. I'm going to come quicker than a virgin on prom night. I lean forward and grip the desk for support as the warm build of release holds me in its clutches. My dick throbs as I come in needy spurts all over the floor between my legs.

I reach over for some napkins from a fast food packet and startle when I feel something touch my ankle. *Meow.* Ginger? What the hell? The feline helps herself to my deposit on the floor. I slap her away and that's when it dawns on me that she couldn't have got in on her own.

I turn to the footsteps behind me and jump up, zipping my fly. Fuck! An aging woman stares back at me, fumbling with a walking stick. "I was just checking the locks." Her jittering arm points to the door. "Some kids broke in a few months back and made a dreadful mess."

I know exactly who she is. She's the only other person that lives within a quarter mile. She's eighty-four and really unlucky to have walked in here because now I can't let her leave.

I approach her slowly. She looks around me at the monitors.

"I'm sorry you came here." I tell her.

Before she can fathom what's happening, I grasp her head and push it backwards against the wall. She crumbles unconscious against my chest. I carry her to a back room and lock her in there.

I call Noah and get his voicemail. "Noah, why do you never answer your phone? This is the emergency number and you still don't fucking answer. I have a blip. I need you to take care of someone. I'm packing up and moving everything now. I left the problem in the back room. It will need to be cleaned." Ending the call, I grab Ginger and shove her out the front door. I should never have fed the fucking thing. They always come back if you feed them.

I pack everything up and stealthily leave.

Nine

NOAH

I shouldn't drink so much. I won't tell Devon I've left this old hag in here for six hours. I need to stay high on the latest mark for as long as possible, which causes me to zone out for long periods of time.

Old people are surprisingly durable. They have lived a long fucking life and survived it, after all. A little gasp leaves her mouth when I enter the room. Devon can't take a life, he's too soft. Killing Courtney broke something inside him, or perhaps that broke the rest of him. Our father had a way of chipping away at him, his main threat. *"If you speak about what happens in this house, I'll open up your meat shirt and show you my fist crushing your traitorous heart."*

Hmm, fond memories.

I grab the old girl by her hair and drag her to her feet. I don't waste time playing with her; she's too frail to enjoy toying with. I snap her neck and sling her over my shoulder. She's heavier than I assumed she'd be.

"Like having biscuits with your sweet tea, huh, Grandma?" I mock, slapping her dead ass.

I dump her at the bottom of the stairs in her own house, hoping her death will look accidental. This shit is unacceptable. He's acting carelessly which isn't like him. This whole fucking mark has him acting weird. The sooner I finish this the better.

Ten

Nina

I SIGH UNDER MY BREATH when I catch Mr. Ilavich peering over the fence to my right. Although he's harmless, he's constantly trying to become friendlier than I really want. At over double my age, I really can't figure out what we would have in common that would merit a friendship.

"Nina?"

I push my sunglasses into my hair, sliding my bangs back on my head, and smile at him. "Good morning Mr. Ilavich."

His eyes roam over my body and my skin blanches in my small bikini. Just once I would appreciate some privacy in my own back yard as I try and get a tan to my pale skin. "Just letting you know I'll be leaving this afternoon for a couple of days."

"Oh, taking a Vacation?" I ask as I can't hold back the smile. My wish has been granted.

He shakes his head. "Not really, just a business trip. I was wondering if you could feed Teddy."

I grimace. Teddy is Mr. Ilavich's Chihuahua, and an evil little shit at that, but he always feeds Ginger when I'm working late so I can't refuse. I nod and force a smile. "Of course."

"You're an angel." I nod and slide down my glasses, hoping he'll take the hint, but he doesn't. "I will only be a couple of days."

I nod again, not giving him the satisfaction of a conversation, but as always, the man is unwavering. "Oh by the way . . ." He pauses and waits. "Nina?"

Once again, I glide my glasses onto my head and look at him. Once again, his gaze creeps over my body then back to my face. "You had a parcel delivered. Just a minute."

He disappears. Grabbing the moment, I hook up my sandals and run into the house, quietly closing the door so he doesn't hear, and run up the stairs. It isn't long before his familiar tap echoes on the glass in the back door. "Nina?"

I hang out of the bathroom window. "I'm sorry, Mr. Ilavich, but I think I've had too much sun. I'm vomiting like a rabid dog." He grimaces which makes my lips twitch. "Can you leave the parcel by the door, please? I'll fetch it in a while." Without waiting for him to answer, I shut the window and giggle to myself at the picture of his face.

I'm not normally rude but my patience is wearing thin. He needs friends his own age.

I give the toilet another flush to make it convincing then leave the bathroom and flop onto my bed. The week has been tiring. One of the girls at the club got the virus that's going around, and because I need the cash, I put my name down for all her shifts. Today is my first day off in ten days and I'm adamant my neighbor is not going to spoil my relaxing time.

Deeming it safe, I venture downstairs, my grumbling belly telling me it's way past lunch time. Cranking up the volume on the music, I pull out some ingredients from the fridge and dance along the tiled floor in bare feet as I prepare a salad. Treating myself to a cold glass of wine, I carry both through to the lounge and sigh in pleasure as the cool room and food bring back my good mood.

My phone rings and I glance at the name displayed. "Oh, God," I grumble when the club's number ruins my previous mood.

"Nina?" Todd screeches down the phone. "Mary hasn't turned in again."

"Really?"

"Mmm. You couldn't cover could you? Unless you're busy with a date or. .?"

Closing my eyes, I grit my teeth. "Nothing that can't happen another time. What time do you need me in?" God he is so nosey and can't take a freaking hint. I really need to toughen up. Although the money is good, I'm exhausted. I had the bug Mary has last week and I'm still trying to build myself back up.

"Thanks, sweetness. Four until midnight. See you later."

"See you later." I sigh into the dead line. "Again!"

Placing my wine on the table, now unable to drink it because I have to drive, I chew on the lettuce like a bear at a slice of rump as I chunter to myself. The image of the shoes I saw in town pop into my head and I purse my lips. "Well, Nina, at least you can afford them now."

Small things.

The club is wild for a Wednesday night. The new DJ Todd employed brings in the crowds from his old place. At nine o'clock, I manage to slide into the back room and grab a quick break.

"Hi, Nina." Todd smiles as I tear off the lid to my water, and chug the liquid down.

"Hey." I return his smile but Todd gives me the creeps. He's been asking me for a date for months but there's something about him that makes my skin crawl. He's always touching me, and whenever I turn around behind the bar, he's there, his close proximity a little alarming.

"You're on 'til closing?"

Shaking my head I snatch up a bag of chips and dive in. "No, just midnight tonight you said."

He nods and smiles wider. "I can get off then. You wanna go somewhere after?"

Trying to stop myself from growling, I give him an

apologetic smile and shoulder shrug. "Sorry, I'm exhausted. Busy week, and I'm still getting over the stomach bug I had."

His face darkens which surprises me. I thought he was used to my rejections by now. He's had enough of them. "I thought you blew off a date to work?"

"I didn't say that, and if I did, that means I wouldn't really be available to date you, right?"

He grabs my wrist, halting me. "Are you dating anyone?"

Peeling his fingers from my wrist, I shove his hand away. "No."

"Oh well, maybe another day then. When you're feeling better?"

I nod faintly. His mood swing is a little concerning, and I try to give him a reassuring smile but he just blew any chance, which was slim to start with. "Sure."

Rolling my eyes when he slams the door behind him, I kick off my heels and lift my feet onto the small wooden table in between the two couches, and rest the back of my head against the sofa.

"You look beat, babe."

I open my eyes and smile at Tricia, my head nodding to confirm her statement. "I am. I'm going to sleep so hard tonight. Ginger can sit on my face and lick my eyeballs as much as he wants because I won't feel anything."

Tricia laughs and sits on the opposite couch. "That cat has absolutely no manners and gets more action out of you than anyone else. What was Todd saying to you? He looked a bit intense."

"He wants to take me to dinner." I shudder. A thought

occurs to me and I groan. "Oh, crap. I have to feed my neighbor's damn dog too because he's gone away."

"Surely that won't take long?" Her tone appears off but I put it down to the busy night, her eyes revealing how tired she is.

I blow out a huff and lift a brow at her. "Are you kidding? The damn thing is the slowest shitter on the planet! He has to pee on all twenty four conifers and then he will wipe his ass on every inch of lawn!"

She chuckles but grimaces. "Can't you leave him 'til morning?"

"Not unless I want to hear him bark all night."

She nods and pouts sympathetically. "No way round it then, Nee. You should tell Todd that you can't cover for everyone."

I nod and slip my shoes back on. "I know. I need to grow some balls."

She cracks a smile and waggles her eyebrows. "That would also get Todd off your back, instead of trying to get you on it. I don't know why he bothers. Now I'm single he can have me on mine." She flicks her hair and pushes her boobs together.

"I didn't have to wait for you to be single for that." His deep voice echoes from behind her, startling me.

Laughing loudly in agreement, she winks at him and I make my way back to the bar, my throbbing feet telling me it's going to be a long night.

Eleven

NOAH

My heart skips when I watch her climb from her car, her long legs encased in a pair of pants that hug her ass. Oh, she's definitely a looker. My cock hardens in preparation for the fight I hope she gives me.

The room light comes on and I grin to myself as she draws the drapes, displaying to me her large tits. Fuck, the night just gets better.

I wait for the bedroom light to come on but after a while, when it doesn't, I climb from the car and make my way closer, avoiding the streetlamps and keeping to the shadowed edges. It's an easy approach; the many shrubs and trees being my associates for the night and offering me sanctuary against the adrenaline coursing through me. The long shadows they give out match my soul, the evil inside me pouring out and aiding my undertaking.

I stop when a figure cuts through the driveway in front of me, its shadow stretching from next door's fence. I know it's her; the shape of her tits in the darkness can't be missed.

"Ssh, Ginger," she whispers.

The hairs on the back of my neck stand to attention with the sound of her soft voice. She's femininity in its element; the fall of her long hair, her tiny waist, and her large breasts. She was created for monsters like me.

The lock clicks on the back door. I smile. I love a challenge and she thinks she can keep me away.

How wrong she is. How wrong they both are. I can see now why my brother is so enthralled with this one. She is quite fucking delectable.

Twelve

Nina

I CAN'T BREATHE. THE DAMN cat is sitting on my face again. I open my eyes and the restriction in my throat worsens when I realize it isn't Ginger pressed against my nose—it's a hand.

Time is frozen for what seems like forever. I can't move. My body won't decipher the messages my brain is trying to thrust into my nervous system. My blood rushes through the tightness of my veins, each cell in my body being shocked with a ferocity my mind is unable to cope with. *I'm not alone. Someone is here with me in my room, suffocating me.*

My eyes widen as they adjust to the darkness. All I can

focus on is the whites of his eyes through his balaclava, the evil reflected back at me through his irises the only thing I can concentrate on.

My heart rate is going through the roof and vomit is rising up my throat but still I can't move. I stare absently up at the man holding me down.

His thighs are thick, each of them clamping my arms by my sides. His breathing is heavy and there's a slight wheeze with each exhalation. His hand is large and gloved, the press of his fingers against my cheekbone harsh and deep.

It's then and only then that I feel the press of his erection in my stomach.

It's then and only then that my brain finally realizes what is happening.

It's then and only then that instinct kicks in and I start to fight.

He holds me harder as I start to flip beneath him, my body bucking violently as I try to free myself from under him. The vomit curls deep in my stomach and tears burn my eyes when I realize what he wants.

"No, please," I mumble around his hand as my head shakes, my body following suit as every inch of me starts to tremble.

"Ssh." His whisper is almost soothing, like he cares that I'm distressed. His eyes soften for a brief second as he tips his head to the side very slightly. "Ssh."

"No!" I start to cry harder as I pull at my hands in attempt to free them. But he's strong, too strong. I know I have no chance against him but I'm damned if I don't try. Opening my mouth, I pull back my lips and bite into the flesh of his hand as hard as I can. He laughs and pulls it back quickly.

Taking the opportunity, I suck in air and scream as loudly as I can. I'm praying Mr. Ilavich hears me. It's only when my attacker punches me in the side of the head that I remember Mr. Ilavich is away.

"You loud little bitch!" he hisses as he stuffs some material into my mouth, both stopping my scream and my ability to bite. "I don't mind a screamer but teeth are a no, no," he snarls, leaning forward and biting into my shoulder. The pain is immense, burning like his teeth are made of lava. Pulling up, his mouth is dripping. Crimson drops land on my face followed by a chunk of my own flesh. "Unless it's me doing the biting," he adds. The purest kind of evil is looking down on me with depravity saturated in every word.

The stupid thing is, all I can think as he binds my hands to the bed is 'Thank God I've gotten over the flu, or I wouldn't be able to breathe.'

There were many strange thoughts to come during his four-hour assault.

He strips me with the touch of a lover; a caress hiding the lie of what he truly is; a monster. His hands travel over my skin, exploring my flesh. He tries to soothe me with gentle shushing sounds as he parts my legs. I fight, forcing them to close but he's stronger than me, pressuring them to open for him.

Sobs burst from my chest as I lay bare to him. This is so different to how he was moments before when he tore into my shoulder with his teeth. I panic when I feel his breath on my navel, travelling down between my spread thighs. He swipes out, tasting me, and I can't stop him. He toys with me, bringing feelings I don't want. I hate my body for betraying me and letting this man elicit any arousal in me but he appears to know how to work my body, to turn it against me. In the most horrific moment of my life, he feasts on me like I'm his lover and the best thing he's ever had on his tongue, his fingers sliding inside me with skill. I'm repulsed, my stomach twisting with the heat of arousal, but unable to stop my body from responding too. It's the worst kind of torture. I hate him . . . I hate myself. I know my body is reacting to an action, stimulation, rather than emotion, but it's still a betrayal, one I'll never forgive myself for. He pulls the material from my mouth.

"You're clenching your dirty fucking cunt, coming all over the place like some cheap slut gagging for attention." He rubs me roughly and then rubs my treachery all over my face. "Taste what your hungry pussy gave me so willingly."

"Fuck you!" I scream, before biting down on his finger. I draw blood, I can taste the iron twang hit my tongue. He quickly pries my jaw apart and I try pulling and kicking to no avail.

His fist impacts the side of my head, making my vision blur. "No, you vile slutty little cunt—fuck you! I'm going to punish you for drawing blood."

The worst part was over, the soft side was more humiliating than the anger, which came next. The pain and brutality of him using anything he could find to rape me with. He hated me with every part of him. His fists rained down whenever my spirit would gain momentum and I tried to fight him off. The tearing and bruising throbbed with such intensity that my mind tried to turn off and take me into the darkness but he wouldn't allow me to go. He used freezing water to bring me around from the dazed state and then took a belt to my tender flesh, the hiss of the air and sharp snap as it lashed against me caused vomit to rise and spill from my mouth. He mocked me and called me cruel names. In the end I didn't focus on the feel of him, or the sounds he made, or even how he moved me many times, at one point dislocating my shoulder when he pulled me so hard, turning me, not caring that the binds wouldn't allow for it. I concentrated on the sound of the rain beating heavily on my window, and the faint howl of the wind that always carried through the attic above my bedroom.

When he untied my wrists and threw me from the bed to the floor, my head thudded brutally on impact. My nails dug into the wooden floorboards as I tried to drag myself away from the soundtrack of his mocking laughter. The tearing of my fingernails being left in the floor as he hauled me back by my ankles was excruciating.

His filthy dick abuses me and spills his fluids inside me, stinging every tear he causes. I know when he coats me in his DNA that he probably plans on killing me. The fear is gone. He uses me up and rapes the fight out of me.

My mind wanders to my childhood, the way my dad would smile at me whenever I managed to complete another curl on my letters, or when I learnt a new word. My mother's happy laughter soothed my soul as she walked with me to school and praised me for all my hard work.

As he forces his hand inside me and tears me apart, I

let myself drift away to my memories.

I remember Sammy, our pet tortoise, and how I would tape Barbie to his back and watch him shuffle around the room with her for a companion. I remember feeding my uncle's Koi in his huge pond. I remember Jimmy, the boy who used to live next door before he drowned in their pool.

I'm drowning now, in the taste of my own blood.

I must have passed out because I can't remember how I ended up in the shower stall on the tiled floor, cold water bringing me round to consciousness. I wish it hadn't. He's emptied my bottles of shower wash and shampoo over me and scrubs at my skin, making sure to clean me thoroughly, and then pushes the head of the shower inside me. I beg him to stop, my throat too raw for my screams to make a sound.

When he's finished, he warns me that he could come back anytime. I don't feel the blood running down my legs, or the pain in my cheek where he hit me time and time again. I don't feel the soreness in my backside or the stinging bites on my chest. All I feel is an overwhelming grief when I fall out my front door to flee and find he's broken Ginger's neck and left her out in the rain.

Thirteen

Nina

Twelve months later

Pulling back the drape slightly, I squint through the glass at the van that pulls up at the front of my house. My heart beats rapidly in my chest as my nerves ramp higher and higher, my mouth drying and making it difficult to swallow. My hand automatically rubs over the scars on my chest.

A tall man climbs out of the driver's side as another, smaller man jumps out from the passenger side. Both wear jeans and a hoody, and both laugh at something the tall one says.

The tall man turns to look at the house, his eyes narrowing as his lip curls in disgust. It's obvious he or his friend have bought it. I'm surprised really. The rundown three story house has been empty since I moved here eleven months ago, and that had been one of the main reasons I purchased it—its remoteness and lack of nosy neighbors. Now it seems my ideal home has been squashed in the three seconds it took the two men to pull up outside.

The man turns his face in my direction, and I let the drape drop back down, my breath catching in my throat at the knowledge he's seen me looking. The light that briefly filtered into the room evaporates, and again, I'm left alone in the dim room. For the eleven months I've been living here, I still can't open the curtains. It's stupid, and I have absolutely no reason to be scared, but my dreams, or rather my nightmares, are full of—*him*, his masked face peering at me through the window as I sleep in the darkness. So now, I leave the lights on and keep the drapes closed, just in case the dreams are not dreams, but premonitions of what's to come. They can't come true if I do everything I can to change them. That's what I figure in the dark recesses of my mind, anyway.

My lungs squeeze tight when I hear a knock on the glass of the front door. It's only light but the shock of it is blazingly loud in my head. I press back against the wall and place a hand over the screaming inside my chest. The disturbance to my heart rate makes me feel lightheaded. I press my other palm to the wall behind me to support the tremble in my legs.

"Go away," I whisper to myself when another knock eerily echoes around the house. "Go away." I plead, but I don't think it's loud enough to be heard.

"Hello?" His loud voice ricochets off every lobe in my brain and I start to hyperventilate when I see his cloudy face press up to the mottled glass at the door.

Steve, my grey fluffy cat, answers his knock with a meow as he trots across the room, seeking me out to wrap his fat body around my shins.

"Not now, Steve. Please." I know, as well as Steve knows, that it's his supper time, and he isn't about to let me off as he twists more furiously around my scrawny legs. His prickly tongue laps at my toes as if he's about to become a cannibal and eat me from the bottom upwards. "Steve!" I hiss when the man's face appears at the window again.

What the hell is his problem? He's relentless! Leave me alone!

"Hello!"

I grit my teeth and push back harder into the wall, praying as I close my eyes that he'll go away.

As if sensing my reluctance to greet him, he backs away, the scrunch of his feet on the gravel driveway calming my nerves the further away he gets.

I blow out a breath of relief and scoop Steve up, burying my face into the thick, soft fur to apologize for not giving him the attention he wants. "I'm sorry, baby. Mommy's coming."

He's the only person that ever has my attention. There's no one else in my life. However that's my own choice, and I intend to keep it that way until God grants me passage into a better place. A place where monsters don't exist and nothing but the sun beats on my soul.

I groan in frustration when I open the cupboard to take out Steve's food and find half a can of soup, and nothing else. "Shit!"

I look down at him, my expression hopeful as I beg him with my eyes that he could starve for the night. "I forgot to order shopping, Steve." His replying meow and nudge of his nose tells me he isn't going to let me off. Apparently he doesn't like to go hungry.

My mouth dries as I snatch up the car keys and slowly walk through the kitchen and into the garage. I glare at Steve as he sits his ass down on the steps and watches me with his own fierce glare. "Traitor!"

I make sure all the doors are locked then flick the switch to raise the garage door and back out. The two men moving in next door turn their heads and stare at me as though I'm an alien with six heads. The small one turns back to what he's trying to lift out of the back of the van, but the tall one fixes me with a stare, his soft features watching me closely as he squints to look at me through the windshield.

I can't close my eyes and hide from him because I'm currently backing onto the road at a speed I've never pushed my little car before. Something in the engine squeals with the effort I'm forcing on the gas pedal. He's still surveying everything around me as I tear off down the road. I can only pray that he's gone when I return, but with my luck, I know he'll still be there, watching for me to return so he can bang on my freaking door again.

The guy behind the counter makes my body shiver when he leers at me as I place the cat food and milk on the counter. He's only young, and harmless more than likely, but it doesn't matter. My own shadow feels like a threat.

"Just those," I say as I keep my eyes away from his.

"Anything else I can get you, doll face?"

I shake my head, studying the change in my wallet like it contains the secrets of the world. "No," I croak. "Thank you."

"You sure?" he asks, oblivious to my urgent need to get the hell out of the store. "We have a good price on condoms at the moment."

I shake my head again and drop the cash onto the side. It bounces then spills over the edge and every single coin disperses into three hundred different directions.

"Freaking hell!" I grate through my clenched teeth. My hands are shaking when I bend to retrieve the money, some coins still spinning on their side as I hurry, snatching them up eagerly. But the last coin is picked up by a different hand.

I remain still, crouched on the floor, as a pair of sneakers come into my line of sight. "You're pushing your luck. What kind of question is that to ask a customer? I'm sorry to your mom but that's the final straw. This is your week's notice," I hear him tell the guy behind the counter.

I know he's waiting for me to stand and take back the ten cents but instead I spin around and fish another out of my wallet, slamming it and the rest of the money onto the counter before I grab my groceries and swiftly shoot out of the store.

"Excuse me!" the man who came to my aid shouts after me, but I'm practically running now, the frantic pace of my heart struggling to feed my veins with blood. My brow is beaded with sweat as I scramble into my car and flick down the locks. My eyes look up to see the shop owner holding his hand out and the local sheriff who I rushed past in my need to flee begins to walk over to my car but I tear out of the car park like there's a damn wolf at my heels.

Tears pool in my eyes and I'm so freaking angry at myself. He was being polite, trying to help me and I was rude. Utterly rude. I hate what I've become, hate myself. Hate what *he* had transformed me into. I once loved life, been happy, and although my career hadn't been taking me anywhere, I had still been content and at ease with everything about me. Now I detest looking at myself in the mirror. All that stares back at me is a hollow shell of horror and a ghost of the past. A ghost that's scared of its own shadow.

I creep along the muddy road as I approach my house, my face pressed to the window when I kill the headlights and try not to attract the attention of my new neighbors. For the first time in a long while, I am lucky. The lights to the house are on, but apart from that, no signs of life meet my return.

Steve greets me excitedly when I rush back into the house and quickly bang shut the adjoining door from the garage, slamming the four bolts home as I turn the two locks.

"I'm here, big guy."

He purrs loudly, wrapping himself around me again

while I tear off the can lid and scoop an extra-large portion into his dish to apologize for the wait.

"Salmon. Your favorite." I beam at him when he jumps up on the countertop and starts to nuzzle my ear. "I love you too," I reply.

I have absolutely no idea how old Steve is. He came to me every night since I moved into the house and I'm sure the previous owners had just upped and left him. In my own twisted mind, I tell myself he's Ginger incarnate. The landlord informed me they had owed a serious amount in rent, a hidden warning to me when he'd told me pointedly with a message in his eyes I'd had no trouble deciphering. He gives me the jitters too. The way he looks at me is beyond the familiarity of acquaintances, like he knows I'm fleeing, and knows the reasons why. However, he's the only person I see. His visits once a month to collect the lease money are the only real face to face conversations I've had with another adult during the previous eleven months—apart from the guy in the store and the delivery man who I snatch bags from and nod my head in thanks. I Skype and talk on the phone so that counts as socializing right?

The phone rings, and giving Steve one last stroke, I leave him to eat in private, and pick up the handset, walking through to the lounge as I answer. "Hey."

I grin to myself when Tricia's soft voice curls around me. "How are you?"

"I'm doing okay," I answer with a slight grimace, knowing exactly what is coming.

"So you're up to visitors now?"

I gulp and shift with discomfort. "Well . . ."

"Oh, bullshit to this, Nina. I'm coming out this Friday

to see you. Make up the spare bed, girlfriend. I'm staying for the weekend, and hopefully I'll drag your sorry ass out for some fresh air!"

"Tricia..."

"Don't 'Tricia' me," she growls, mimicking my quiet voice. "I haven't seen you since you left. You've made excuse after excuse. Well, now I'm sick of your stupid excuses. I miss my friend. Todd keeps asking for your number."

"No, don't!"

"Oh, don't panic. I wouldn't do that. Anyway, he has some fucking balls. He asks after fucking me senseless about getting my best friend's number? I'm going to have to fuck his best friend now to teach him a lesson."

"That's really insensitive of him. I hate men."

"Yeah, well I hate them too, except I love their cocks and fingers and tongues, and occasionally their asses when I find one open to being pounded in the back door." She giggles down the line.

"Todd?" I ask with a gasp.

"Oh, God, no. I wish. He likes to do the back door pounding. I've told him you're too fucked up to be into anything like that so I don't get why he pursues you."

I'm shocked silent by her statement. Static crackles across the line and after a few awkward silent beats, she says, "Shit. I didn't mean that how it came across. I'm so sorry. Nee, I just meant you aren't his type."

I inhale a shaky breath and tell myself to breathe.

"Nee?"

"It's fine."

Steve saunters into the room, his tongue lapping at the clumps of salmon stuck to the fur around his mouth. His grey eyes settle on me and I'm sure he quirks a damn eyebrow at me and sighs in exasperation, judging me silently for my behavior.

Closing my eyes and already regretting it, I concede. "Okay, I'll fix up the spare bed."

"YAY!" she squeals causing me to hold the phone a little away from my ear.

Truth be told, I have missed my best friend, and something in the air tonight makes me want to feel her tight hug and see her pretty smile.

She is silent for a moment then she sighs heavily. "I'll be there about four. Make sure you have wine chilling and a hot pizza delivery guy on standby."

I can't help but laugh. "Okay, I'll see you Friday."

My smile is wide when I end the call but the rampant beat in my heart belies that happiness as anguish coils deep in the pit of my belly. I know Tricia will be shocked by what has become of her best friend. I'm no longer curvy and bold. My skin isn't soft and full of life anymore, nor is my spirit high and bright. Now I'm gaunt and thin, my voice a mere whisper and my body stiff with tension and strain.

I haven't seen her since she hugged me hard and sobbed that she loved me before I had climbed into my little car and left. I never returned, and to be honest, I never want to. Nina is gone, and the girl that remains in her place is a living corpse that holds the previous owners eyes; the only thing that remains of the old me. The me before my life ended in a single night.

The phone shrills in my hand as soon as I hang up. "What now?" I ask rolling my eyes, knowing she probably forgot to tell me about a conquest or something.

"Ma'am, this is Sheriff Logan."

My heart thuds heavily in my chest. "How did you get this number?" I ask meekly.

"I'm the sheriff," he states and I hear humor in his voice. "I'm calling to check in on you. I would drive over but you appeared to be in a hurry somewhere."

"My cat needed to be fed."

"Eh? Okay, well you should take care when driving Ma'am, I'm sure your . . . cat would prefer you made it home in one piece."

"Okay," I whisper.

"Are you sure you're alright? I can come by if there's something you need or want to tell me?"

"No, no, I don't. I'm fine. Please don't come here."

"Okay, well stay safe and I hope you and your cat enjoy your dinner."

I hang up the phone and cry. There's no explanation for the tears other than my shame for being so freaking messed up.

Fourteen

I WATCH MY NEIGHBOR AS I sit at the window. It's been two days since he's moved in and this is the first time since the first encounter that I've seen him again. He's up a ladder, painting the front of the house, his long legs having no trouble helping him reach the high areas.

"Nina?"

I turn back to the laptop perched on the table in the middle of the room. Heather's soft features smile back at me via our Skype video chat. "I'm listening," I lie.

She raises both brows then smirks at me. "I think there is something more entertaining outside than our chat."

I shrug then drop back the drape and settle myself around, giving my therapist my full attention. "Tricia is visiting today."

Her eyes widen but her grin tells me she's pleased with this revelation. "Good." She nods eagerly. "It will do you good to have some adult conversation."

"You mean other than you." I smirk.

She smiles softly. "How long has it been since you've seen your friend?"

"Since the day I came here."

She nods but continues to smile at me. "Do you think you can be open with her?" She nods again when I shake my head. "But Tricia does know of the attack?"

"She knows," I answer, the nosy woman who has become more a friend than therapist "But she doesn't know the extent of it." A shiver rages through my body and I wince.

"Maybe you'll find it therapeutic to talk to her."

I scoff. "I doubt that very much. But knowing Tricia, she'll be more interested in the local gossip, and if there are any hot men around."

Heather laughs. "Well, just try and enjoy her visit."

A knock at the back door makes my throat suddenly ache. "She's here," I whisper to Heather as my nerves ramp my heart beat higher.

"Take a deep breath, Nina." I try to smile at her attempt to calm me but then figure it's her job to tell me everything will be okay when I know I will never be okay again. "She's your friend. You need to tell your mind that. Our previous discussion would be helpful here. Not everyone is an enemy."

"Aren't they?" I choke out when another knock makes my skin chill.

"No, Nina. They're not. Now go and let her in, but

promise me you will at least try and be open with your friend. She's your friend for a reason and I think you'll find that she's more concerned about you than you realize."

I roll my eyes as I shut the laptop, ending our call abruptly. My palms are sweating as I take hold of the door handle and pull open the door. My legs tremble, and for a moment I can't breathe when my neighbor stands smiling at me. But then my eyes drop to Steve in his arms. Well, I think it's Steve. His grey fur is now dyed a severe bright white, his blue eyes the only thing left of him that's original. "Steve!"

My neighbor cringes, causing me to lift my eyes back to him. "I'm so sorry. The can of paint fell from my ladder and I didn't realize your cat was lying beneath it."

I can't talk as my mouth dries and my ears begin to hum. I'm staring at him while he waits for me to say something. He bites on his bottom lip and scrunches his nose. It's placid and endearing, and for unknown reasons it calms my severed nerves.

"Are you okay?" he asks as his eyes soften with concern.

A shiver rages through me with the sound of his quiet voice. Something about it makes my heart beat faster and my gut clench. He looks at me quizzically and repeats his question.

I nod quickly and step backwards when he reaches out to me. "Sorry," I choke out, coughing to clear my throat when he frowns at me. "I'd better get Steve bathed before the paint dries."

He grimaces again and nods. "I'm so sorry."

I shake my head as I take Steve from him and scowl at

the damn feline. He's always getting himself into trouble, even in the near vicinity of his home where there's nothing but open fields and an old rundown windmill. But he keeps the field mice away, so he more than pays for his upkeep. "It's no problem."

He smiles and I blink when his features completely change. His eyes light, reflecting every single piece of his delight, and a small dimple appears in his chin, my eyes roving over his face until they settle on it. "I . . ." He pauses and I shift my gaze back up his eyes. I'm beginning to relax, even managing a small smile when he grins at me. "I noticed that you have a loose gutter. I can take a look at it if you want, while I've got my ladders out."

"Uhh." I scratch my head and swallow when another wave of nerves floors my heart rate. I've been asking my landlord for three months to fix it and I'm still waiting. When it rains hard the water drips through the rubbish sealant around the window frame and my drapes are always having to be washed.

"It's not a problem," he says when he senses my apprehension.

"Well, uhh, I'm not sure how I can pay."

He tuts and shakes his head. "Don't be silly. It's the least I can do after what I've done to poor Ginger."

I drop Steve to the floor and bile rises in my throat. My vision distorts and I hear a loud buzzing in my ears. "His name is Steve. Why did you call him Ginger?" Tears pool and leak down my cheek. I flinch and smack his hand away when he reaches out for me.

"Shh, calm down. It's okay, it's okay. Damn, you're shaking. I can hear you rattling. It's okay, I would never hurt you."

"Why did you call him that?" I demand.

"You called him that," he states with conviction. I feel shame and regret crawl through my veins.

"I'm sorry."

"It's okay, really. Please don't feel frightened of me."

"It's my go-to response. I'm so sorry, I'm a freak, I know." I half laugh with no humor.

This is getting ridiculous. Everyone will label me a weirdo and come for me with torches and pitchforks soon.

"You're not a freak. I painted your cat and you no doubt inhaled some of the toxins. Again, I'm sorry for that, and please let me fix your guttering."

I swallow and then nod. "Thank you."

He beams at me, the white of his teeth attracting my attention. "No thanks needed . . ." He hesitates as he waits for my name.

"Sarah." I whisper the first name that comes into my head.

He frowns slightly but then blinks, as if to shake himself out of his pondering. He thrusts his hand out, encouraging me to take it. I stare at it for a moment, and before I embarrass myself further, I brace myself and slip my hand into his, my bones vibrating at the connection to another human being after so long. "It's a pleasure to meet you, Sarah. My name's Devon."

Devon, I like that.

I smile at his happy tone. He genuinely seems nice and I push back the nerves, the constant reminder of my past now angering me. "And you, Devon."

He gives me a wink as he drops my hand then walks

away. "I'm sure we'll be great friends as well as neighbors," he shouts over his shoulder before he disappears around the corner of his house.

I don't reply. I'm still smiling, proud of myself for biting my cowardice and braving out the confrontation with another, and even if I did go a little crazy on him, he doesn't appear to mind. Maybe things are finally looking up.

And my mood improves when I hear Tricia's Mustang convertible roar up the driveway. Life is suddenly that little bit better. And I pray it continues on that path.

"Are you serious?" I scoff, shaking my head and laughing at Tricia as we sit on the decking and enjoy a bottle of wine in the late afternoon sun.

She nods, smirking at me. "Oh yes." Pinching her forefinger and thumb together, she squints at the tiny space between them. "Tiny. I'm telling you, the man needs surgery on that nugget."

I smile and take another sip of wine. It's good to be able to smile again. Blinking, I notice Tricia smiling back at me. "It's so good to see you, Nee. I've missed you so much."

"I know," I whisper, unable to raise my voice any higher with the flux of emotion rushing through me as I look at me friend. "I'm sorry."

She nods but still smiles. "You thought any more

about coming home?"

Looking up to the sky, I sigh. "There's something you need to know . . ."

"Oh my fucking God," Tricia whispers. "Why didn't you tell me how hot your neighbor is?" She narrows her eyes at me. "No wonder you don't wanna come home, girl. You man hogging bitch!"

I peer at her in confusion for a second before I follow her line of sight. Devon is standing in his garden, the lack of fencing between our two houses showing off his topless body as he tends to some weeds. I turn away quickly, downing another large mouthful of wine. Tricia is openly ogling him and I feel my cheeks heat with her blatant gawping. "Trish!"

She ignores me, and when she calls out, I slide down the chair in sheer embarrassment.

"Well, hello there!"

Devon turns, but the lack of surprise on his face tells me he already knew we were there.

"Hi!" He looks our way and I blink at the timid smile. "Lovely day!" he calls as he shields his eyes from the sun and directs his gaze to me.

I smile and nod politely then shift round slightly. Tricia, in all her glorious bikini clad body, thrusts her boobs out as she lifts her glass of wine. "You look a little hot. Would you care for a glass?"

"TRISH!" I hiss under my breath, and pull my cardigan tighter around my body.

"What?" She gawps at me then shrugs when she sees my horror. "He's your neighbor. I doubt he's gonna surprise us with a samurai sword down his pants. Although, shit, looking at that bulge, he definitely has some sort of sword down there!" She squints at him. "He looks a little familiar. Maybe I've already dipped my toe in that pool."

"How would you not remember? Damn how many men do you go through?"

She shrugs. "I'm trying to find the one."

"One of many."

"Damn straight! I'm single. No harm in sampling the many to find the right fit."

"Gross, Trish. You've only been single for a few months. How many could you have possibly had?"

"Twelve."

"Twelve men?"

"Twelve months. I've been single over twelve months, the same amount of time you've been hiding out here."

I don't have time to think about what she's said because hot, half naked neighbor blocks out the sun.

"Oh dear God," I mumble as he strolls across his garden, climbs over the small wall that is supposed to declare the point of separation between the two houses then lowers himself onto the top step of the decking and reaches out for the wine Tricia hands him. I can't help but stare at the way his abs move, the sweat he's worked up with gardening trickling down between his monstrous pecs. His right nipple is pierced and I swallow back the dryness in my mouth when my eyes land on his hip bones showing above the waistband of his low blue jeans.

"Steve seems to approve of my flowerbed." Devon smirks at me. "He seems to think my roses need some more manure."

My mouth falls open in embarrassment. "Oh my God,

I'm so sorry." He laughs and waves my apology away.

"He's a cat. They don't understand that it's not polite to shit on folks' flowers. Besides, you never know, it might do them good. God knows they need all the help they can get. The earth here is really arid and lacks the nutrients they need to thrive."

Trish is gawping at him like he just told her his dick size broke all Guinness world records. Her eyes are wide and the way her chest is heaving is making me blush. "You're a keen gardener?" I ask, trying to divert his attention away from my shameless friend.

He smiles at me and it's so very real. One thing I've come to learn over the past years is how fake some people really are. They can say one thing but their facial expressions, especially their smiles, say something entirely different. But Devon's smile is radiant, and directed at me as though it is just for me. "Very. That's one of the things that attracted me to the house; its land. Although I wish I would have thought to do a soil test first."

I grimace and cast an eye over my own plot of land. "As you can tell, I'm awful with plants. I don't seem to be able to not kill them!"

He laughs, the deep timbre making Tricia sigh dreamily. I roll my eyes and smile awkwardly at Devon when he blinks curiously at my friend.

"I could help you if you want," he offers. "We can start with hardy plants. It's very therapeutic, spending time in the garden. Nature's gifts can be stimulating and very soothing to the soul."

Tricia's eyes widen, and from the look on her face I can tell she's suddenly gone off him. His obvious passion for the environment is cute and I smile warmly at him, glad that my friend seems to have changed her mind quickly. "Thank you. That would be good. God knows I could use the help."

He smiles widely. I'm shocked by my acceptance of him but my instincts aren't screaming, and for once I throw caution to the wind and decide to give him a chance. I can learn to trust them, right?

"Well, that's if we can keep Steve away for long enough." He winks then drains his glass of wine. "Well, thank you, ladies." He hands the glass back to Tricia then nods his head and leaves us alone again.

"I definitely don't know him. He seems . . . nice," Tricia remarks.

"Nice is good." I scowl at her.

"Nice is boring," she retorts with a pout. "We girls need someone with a bit of excitement in them."

"Trish! Just because he likes plants doesn't mean he isn't exciting."

She chuckles and shakes her head. "You have a lot to learn, Nee. You should start by taking off your sleep suit when the sun is glorious."

"It's an all in one pantsuit not a sleep suit." I scrunch my nose up at her.

"It's practically a habit."

"A habit?"

She rolls her eyes and takes a big swig from the fresh glass of wine she's just poured. "It's what nuns wear, and no man wants to get under those drapes."

I roll my eyes, ignoring her comment. She's the type of girl who always needs a man in her life, or rather, a man's penis. She isn't bothered about another relationship; she had never been into her last relationship until he cheated with the neighbor.

Shrugging, she settles her gaze back on Devon as he continues with his gardening. "I'd still do him though."

I nod to myself and snort. Of course.

I sigh in irritation and roll over again, desperate to find a cool spot on the bed sheet. It's too warm, the night temperature much the same as the day's now that summer is in full swing. Kicking the duvet to the floor, I huff like a child.

Tricia is giggling in the bedroom next to mine. I can tell she's on the phone to someone; the thin walls notifying me that she's flirting shamelessly with a guy who she has on speakerphone, my ears unable to hear anything else apart from their dirty conversation.

When I hear a gruff groan, I shiver; the knot forever present in my gut tightens and coils. I climb from my bed. I do not want to hear them having internet sex or phone sex, or whatever the hell she's into now. How she can think about anything other than the house cooking us alive is beyond me. Because of my attack, anything sexual makes my stomach turn, so I press play on my iPod and turn the volume to low, just enough to disguise Tricia and co.

Pulling the thin drapes back, I push the window open further, trying to tempt a little more air into the stifling heat of my room.

My gaze goes straight to my neighbor's house. I can't help it; his main bedroom faces mine, the small gap between the houses doing nothing for the privacy between each house. And he is in his bedroom. He has the ceiling light on, illuminating the space. I know because of this, and my lack of lighting, he can't see me watching him. I'm being a creeper but I can't not watch him. It's like gravity is pulling my eyes to him, forcing me to see. He's laid on his bed, his back leaning against a large wooden headboard. He's wearing shorts, his torso naked as his concentration is directed at an open laptop perched on the bed beside him.

I study him for a moment, my curiosity making me feel strange, awakening slight desire mixed with pure inquisitiveness. After a year of being alone, his sudden presence feels peculiar but if I was honest with myself his presence was oddly welcome. I'm so used to being the only one out here in the hills. My nearest town and neighbor are at least two miles away. So now I have company, I can't figure out how I honestly feel about it but for now I'm not running or scared of this new company.

I still instantly and my heart rate increases when his hand moves to his shorts and he starts to rub himself over the top of the tight blue cotton, his erection clearly exposed when the outline of his cock is stroked by his own hand.

"Shit," I whisper to myself, my head turning to make sure I'm still alone and Tricia hasn't suddenly appeared.

When his fingers push down the waistband of his shorts, I know I should look away, pull the drapes and leave him to it, but oddly, I can't. My throat starts to close in, my mouth drying when his cock springs free from the confines of his underwear.

"Oh, crap!"

Yet, still I can't remove my eyes from his pleasuring, his caress mesmerizing as he curls his fingers around the thick shaft and his hand begins to glide up and down smoothly. My breath hitches as fluid suddenly coats my mouth. My lower belly throbs and I hate the way it feels when my nipples harden, pushing against the thin material of my tank and stimulating them further.

What the hell is happening to me?

Fifteen

Devon

I WATCH HER TOSSING AND turning in bed. Her beauty, even in the dark confines of her bedroom is hypnotic. Her every move is displayed to me via my laptop. I'd been lucky the other night when she'd run to the store, giving me a quick chance to slip in and plant a couple of cameras. One in her bedroom and the other in her kitchen. The new wireless cameras that connect to my laptop via GPS were heaven sent, the fact that they didn't need installing a godsend when it had taken me mere minutes to set them up rather than the usual few hours that wired ones do.

I missed her more than I ever knew I could miss anyone. I'm so tethered to her that when that was cut, it was like choking on my own sin. I lived in two worlds; mine and Noah's, and mine and Nina's. I'd hoped to keep them apart, asked for him to let me keep her, but Noah doesn't possess empathy. He doesn't know love or compassion, and my own is more a weakness to him than it is to me.

"This is the life we were born into, Devon. There is nothing else for us. You can't have both."

And he was right. My worlds collided, causing mass destruction. Noah is a snowstorm; cold, isolating, and deadly. And I had to make a choice; I couldn't be in both worlds so I'll live in one. Hers.

Seeing her today with her best friend made me feel disjointed. It's tough learning to be me and stepping out from behind the lens. I'm letting myself have a life but I'm so detached from the world around me, living in it is difficult. I've always relied on Noah for everything. He made me who I am, so to be without him is like my shadow tearing free and running off to live its own story. I keep myself to myself, quickly learning that I don't actually like people much. I find most people self-absorbed. The one I only find engaging, because he's like me in a way, is my friend, Chris. Me, a friend? He was an orphan from the age of fourteen and was raised by an uncle with unorthodox methods of parenting. Chris and I met in a bar and bonded over a barmaid who was trying to seduce us. We took her to a hotel and I fell into old habits, filming her while Chris pushed her sexual limits. It was consensual, but to me it all felt too familiar for comfort. We didn't share any other nights like that, but a kinship was formed nonetheless. He helped me move here and didn't ask questions, which makes for the perfect friendship.

I'm drawn back to Nina as she opens the drapes and pushes open the window opposite mine, the moon illuminating her every move. Her perfect tits push out when her chest lifts and she inhales a breath of fresh air. Just as she's about to move back into the bedroom, she hesitates when she notices me. I swallow, fighting with myself not to look up in her direction and see if I can see her in her physical form instead of the replica image displayed on my laptop screen, although the artificial vision of her still makes my dick hard and my heart constrict.

A wicked thought comes into my head and I have to bite my tongue to stop myself from smiling. Desperation to seek her reaction and to push her into experiencing something natural and beautiful again without disgust and guilt urges me on. Pressing a couple of keys on the laptop, the software brings her image closer so I can catch a more detailed view of her reaction when I slip my hand over my stiff cock. Knowing she's there, our roles reversed as she watches me from the shadows, makes me almost erupt before touching.

She freezes, her beautiful eyes widening as she takes a look back into her bedroom as if checking she's still alone. Her perfect body is rigid and tense, her lips parted to accommodate her deep breaths when she realizes what I'm doing.

It feels unusual being spied on. It amuses me and I stifle a chuckle as I slip down the waistband of my shorts and free my throbbing dick. Watching her, watching me is turning me on as much as having my dick buried inside an eager pussy, my fingers simulating the feeling of a dry cunt.

Sex for me is always about the act. Noah teased me for years about being a virgin in high school. When I was fourteen he made one of his many girlfriends suck my dick; the pleasure was incredible and addictive. I only lasted around forty seconds but it was long enough to embed the craving for sexual release, one Noah made sure I fulfilled. Sex was always a selfish act for me until her. All I cared about was my own release, and giving orgasms was to nurture my own ego. Never before Nina had I wanted to experience her pleasure just to live in the grace of her liberation.

Observing Nina's face closely, I spit on my hand and once again take my cock in its grip. Her jaw opens further, her arousal evident as her nipples peak out from under the thin cotton of her tank. Damn, she's stunning when she's turned on. I expect her to quickly shut the drapes and move back after what Noah did to her, but I hope she's overcome the brutality and learned to separate the difference between sexual release and gratification, and rape, depravity and evil.

I hate him for what he did to her. I begged him not to do it. I'd never asked him for anything, but as with everything our whole lives, Noah was boss.

Twelve months earlier

I wake from the intoxicated sleep I forced myself into last night. I'm not one to turn to the bottle for comfort or relief but I needed it. I severed a bond last night, the only one I'd known for so long, now it's all I know. Noah refused me when I asked him to ignore every rule we promised when starting our business. He refused to go back on the deal and let me keep Nina. I told him I would kill him if he touched her, and he declared that if I didn't allow him to finish the job, that would be the end. He didn't expect me to agree this *is* the end; everything has changed for me, nothing changed for him. He lied when he left me a voicemail telling me I could have her. Or maybe it wasn't a lie. He didn't tell me she would be intact, after all. My insides scream at the file laid out in front of me when I pull myself together. My eyes blur and try to refocus, fear of what lays before me keeping me frozen in my seat. My heart cracks and thumps hard in my chest.

Client—1325

Mark-
Name—Nina Francis Drake
Age—24
Address—126 Lime Ave

Brief—Rape—vaginal—anal
Personal recorded surveillance.
Pain—high
Record assault.—Yes
Courtesy call—No.

Roles.
Client—No
Noah—Contact—Rape.

Devon—No contact—document.

Case—complete. 1325 closed.

Blood stains the paper printout, and bloodied clothes lay next to it. He was in here while I slept. He broke our number one rule. We were to never be in the same place at the same time. In the worst scenario, our world could come tumbling around us by the police, and us not living together limits the chance that they would catch us both, leaving the other to destroy evidence.

Was he setting me up? No, he would never let anyone take the credit for his work.

Moving the bloodied clothes from the table, a note falls to the floor.

You wanted her? You can have her . . . broken.

My feet carry me over to the computer; he disabled the cameras in her house, removing the evidence, but added to the open file I kept of her. My fingers hover, hesitating over the enter key. I gather my balls and push the button.

Her beautiful body lies on her bathroom floor, bloodied, bruised, and spoiled by the beast. I hate him. My blood roars and rebels being related to him. I've witnessed evil in its truest form in my father; he was sin incarnate and his dark, ugly evil corrupted Noah. But despite everything, Noah had never hurt me before this. Looking at Nina, her once blonde hair now red, I know there are no lines, no bonds, and no limits he won't forsake to act out the hate infected inside him. He didn't just break her, he broke something inside me too; the love and admiration I'd always bestowed upon him.

I make an anonymous call for an ambulance and make my way to the last address I have for Noah, but it's barren. He's cleaned out and left me before I can him, and he stole the only thing I wanted. Nina. By the time I'd return, she's discharged herself and left town with no breadcrumbs to follow.

Present Day

It took me a long time to find her, and I plan on never losing her again. However, I know I have to take things slowly with her. Noah left her on the brink of death, her emotional scars as deep as the physical ones. It has been twelve months since I spoke to my own brother. I won't lie and say I don't miss him because I do. He's the only family I have left, but he's gone too far, his greed for depravity and the money it brings more valuable than me. Therefore, I had our relationship severed but I'm not a fool. I knew he'll soon come back into my life, especially if he knows I've tracked Nina down again. Happiness or normal is not something he ever plans to let me have because he himself was never offered that luxury. We were created by a beast and taught to embrace the brutality of its nature.

My thoughts come back to Nina as she hesitantly sits on her window seat and continues to watch me. I'm almost proud of her, her sexuality finally making an appearance after so long. By the overheard conversations with her friend I know she's been living alone all this time. Isolated and frozen in her life.

Taking my attention away from the laptop display, I can't help but imagine it's Nina's fingers embracing my cock, her touch soft but so fucking good. My eyes drift closed as my fist tightens its hold. She's on her knees before me, her wide eyes looking up at me reverently as she strokes me with long hard pulls. Her tongue peeks out, the tip of it tasting the cum that spills from me. She holds my gaze as her lips part and the warmth of her mouth envelopes my whole shaft, her throat gripping the head of my cock when I grab her hair and pull her harder to me. I hear her gag as I pump my hips faster, her retch making my balls shrivel in glorious agony the further my cock descends down her tight little throat.

Her eyes bulge when I slide a hand from her hair and wrap her throat in my fist, her mouth still worshipping me as her airway is completely restricted. But still she sucks hard, her cheeks flushing as I watch her eyes glaze over in lust, in trust that I won't harm her like he did. I'll worship her.

Just as I feel her throat move with her attempts to breathe, I roar out my orgasm and flood her throat, mouth and belly with so much spunk I know she has difficulty swallowing it all, stopping her from taking the breath she so needs to take after my hand blocked off her supply.

I can hardly breathe as cum sprays the length of my stomach in sticky ribbons, the force of my ejaculation so intense that my chest stutters with pain when my ribs compress my lungs forcefully. Snapping my eyes open, remembering what I'm doing, I'm amazed to find Nina with her hand down her own shorts, the camera displaying her frantically rubbing herself.

"Come on, baby. Do it for me," I whisper as I continue to slowly stoke myself, giving her the glory she needs to bring herself off. "Come for me, Nina."

As if hearing me, her head falls back and her mouth opens, a silent scream bursting from her in her own fierce climax, her beauty amplified in the throes of her pleasure.

I have her. I now know that she wants me, otherwise she would have walked away instead of watching me masturbate. But I still have to be careful. The worse thing I can do now is scare her off. But I smile to myself as I shut down the laptop.

She's mine alright. It's just a matter of patience.

Sixteen

Nina

TRICIA GLANCES MY WAY AGAIN, her eyes assessing and probing. I move away and examine a blue dress that hangs in the window of a nearby store. Tricia dragged me begrudgingly to the nearest town, and my nerves very nearly gave me a coronary, but as the hours passed I became more and more at ease.

"Something is different about you today," Tricia mumbles when she comes to stand beside me, her eyes admiring the dress too.

I shrug, leaving my gaze on the unrealistic size zero mannequin in the window. "Well I don't know what."

I know exactly what but I'm as reluctant to face it as

I am to tell her. I can't understand what happened last night, or comprehend what finally brought back my sexual appetite, but I don't like it, not one bit. The orgasm that had taken my breath had both gratified me and disgusted me. My skin had crawled as it simultaneously broke out in goose bumps when the pleasure tore through me. My mind had rejoiced at the bliss that poured through me while my heart ached with memories. The heat that had overpowered my belly had once again turned to loathing when the ecstasy subsided, leaving me weeping into my pillow.

I know I have to move on but my head will never let me. My soul died that day and my fragile heart misses its companion. The scars inside and out forever etched in my

. . .

I scream when a large hand lands on my shoulder. I spin around, whimpering, until I catch Devon looking at me with a frown line creasing his forehead and dropped eyes searching his shoes.

"I'm so sorry." He gulps. "I didn't mean to scare you." He looks utterly contrite; his perfect teeth pop out to worry his bottom lip. I slap a hand over my roaring heart and my wide eyes water.

I can't help but chuckle at my own reaction as my heart rate returns to normal. He grins sheepishly at me when I shake my head in apology. "No, I'm sorry. I was miles away."

He studies me, and although his eyes travelling over every inch of my body is done in a casual manner and mimicked by my own sweep of his torso, I feel his, like a long, slow graze, a caress piercing through the clothing and heating the flesh beneath.

"Hope it was somewhere nice," he murmurs, I blink at him. Was I somewhere nice? It's only then that my brain kicks in and I remember what I was thinking about. My cheeks flush with heat when the image of him, cock in hand and cum squirting across his belly, dances into my head.

"Uhh, very nice." My eyes widen with my impulsive answer, even shocking myself when I realize I'm absent-mindedly flirting with my neighbor. What the hell is going on?

As if sharing the secret, a smirk crosses Devon's face and his eyes twinkle. "Then you must let me join you next time."

He isn't to know he already shares this one with me.

I cough, my whole body now blushing as the context of his words make new images in my head.

"We were just going for lunch. Join us?" Tricia cuts in. It's not really a question. I forgot she's with me. I turn and glare at her but she smiles widely at Devon and points to a bar outside the shop door and across the street. "Ooh, that looks good enough."

I stare after her as she waltzes ahead towards the door, ignoring my silent pleas. One day I'm going to kill her—painfully and satisfyingly.

"Shouldn't you pay for that first?" he asks Tricia, pointing to the blue dress in her arms that she insisted would go with my complexion.

Tossing it on the shelf as she passes, she absentmindedly mumbles, "No. She wouldn't wear it with her scars anyway."

I freeze at her insensitive words spoken so flippantly to a practical stranger. His eyes turn back to me and he shakes his head. Holding out his hand, he asks, "Are you coming?" He pauses mid-step between me and the exit.

Nodding, I force a smile and allow him to lead the way as I cuss my best friend under my breath.

A couple of hours and four bottles of wine later, my vision is slightly blurred as my mouth attempts to vocalize what I'm telling it to say. However, my lips seem to be having a private conversation with my mind and forming new words that have never appeared in the dictionary.

I point a finger at Tricia, her eyes a little wonky as she struggles to focus on me. "Did you spike my lunch?"

She barks out a laugh. "Yeah, with alcohol."

Devon smirks beside me, his eyes laughing at my inability to talk. "I think you might have corrupted her," he says to Tricia.

Her eyes widen and she laughs harder. "I'll have you know, this girl has been the cause of many of our drunken ... *misdemeanors*."

Devon smiles but shakes his head. "Nah, you can't tell me Sarah is to blame for ..."

"Sarah?" Tricia echoes as we both stare at Devon in confusion. "Who the hell is Sarah?"

He looks at us in bewilderment and amusement. "Don't tell me you're so drunk you can't remember your name?"

Tricia gives him a weird look. "Of course not. I'm Tricia Bentley, and this is my best friend, Nina Drake."

He blinks at me. "I thought your name was Sarah?"

Something filters into my mind but I can't grab it. I shake my head. "Nooo, I'm definitely Nina." I look down at myself. "Well I think so."

Tricia snorts and slaps my arm. "But you wish you were Taylor Swift."

"God, no!" I grumble, looking at her in disgust. "Taylor is sickly sweet and every boyfriend cheats on her, or leaves her, or . . ."

Tricia nods firmly. "Well then, you're definitely not Taylor Swift. My best friend used to be the dirtiest tramp on the block."

I'm sure she's mistaking me for herself, unless I'm a slut when I'm drunk and can't remember being one . . . huh?

"Used to be?" Devon questions as he quirks an eyebrow in amusement at his inebriated lunch dates.

Used to be.

My heart plummets and I close my eyes. I'd been having such a good time, my friends making me forget the past. As if sensing the shift in mine and Tricia's moods, Devon becomes somber, his head tilted slightly to one side as he regards me softly. "What happened?"

My mouth opens but when my tongue moves to form words, my misery won't let them loose. It's like they're glued to the inside of my mind, the cage they're kept in keeping my life imprisoned in perpetual unhappiness. I've never opened up to anyone other than my therapist. Even Tricia doesn't know the extent of my attack. She knows

I was beaten and raped but she doesn't know how dark and macabre it actually was. Truth be told, I'm ashamed. Ashamed to admit what *he* did to me. How messed up is that? Not only did the man rape my body, but he raped my life, took over my mind, and controlled my existence ever since. I know, deep down, that I'm allowing him to win, and as much as I've tried to move on, I can't. The chains secured to me prevent me from escaping. I don't know why he chose to come into my home that night. Why me? I may never get the answers, and that keeps me frightened and alone inside my own head.

"Just life," I finally grate out.

Tricia sighs sadly and nods. "Life is grade A bullshit. You're either eager to spread 'em and the man's not interested, or you're not interested and he forces you to spread 'em."

"Trish, that's a freaking shitty thing to say."

Her mouth drops and then her face contorts into a pout. "I'm such a shitty friend," she murmurs as a tear slips from her eyes and races down her face.

Her sorrow becomes mine and I reach out for her. "Hey," I whisper as I take her hand and manage a soft smile. "You're here to show me a good time, sister."

She pulls her shoulders back and nods resolutely then picks up her glass. "And I am. Here's to better times, long friendships, and happiness!"

We all clink glasses, yet I can't help but cast a glimpse at Devon. His brow is furrowed from our odd exchange, but catching me looking, he smiles widely and tips his own glass as he repeats Tricia's toast. "To long friendships and the family we choose."

I smile, nodding to confirm his statement. It's a strange feeling but I somehow know we will become friends. And as much as that makes me anxious, it also gives me hope that things are looking up.

Seventeen

I'M STANDING IN THE MIDDLE of my room. My heart rate is elevated so much it's making me dizzy as my eyes flick from one dark corner to another, my body spinning in circles as my feet scramble around in the pile of the carpet.

I'm being watched.

My skin prickles with awareness as I take a small step backwards, until my back is pressing against the wall. My whole body is alight with recognition, *his* smell, the faint whisper of *his* breathing, *his* badness seeping into the marrow of my bones.

"What do you want?" I choke out, my voice small with terror. "What do you want?" I hate that he has this much control over me.

My head is turning left and right, my eyes trying to peer through the dark room to ascertain his whereabouts. But I can't see him. I can't see him; he lives in the shadows, taunting me.

"Please," I whimper. My chest is heaving, my lungs trying to keep up with the frantic pulls of air as I start to hyperventilate. "Please." My head is shaking so much that the action causes the muscles in my neck to lock and drive pain through my skull. I'm so frightened my bladder threatens to empty. I'm weak, and no one can save me from him.

I press as far back into the wall as I can, my huge eyes blurring as tears hinder my vision. I can't see. I need to see. However, when I do see, I don't want to.

The scream that rushes from me when he steps out from behind the drape makes the drumbeat of my heart the only thing my mind is able to concentrate on. His face is there. *He* is there. Inches from me.

"Oh, God," I weep, my fingers scratching at the wall behind me as I try to dig my way through it. Terror controls my actions, the sheer imminence of him destroying what little courage I found to face him with.

His eyes scorch into me. I know he's smiling even though I can't see his whole face through the mask he's wearing. But I *know* he's smiling.

"Hello again, Nina."

A whimper is all I can manage now as I start to sink down the wall, my sobbing uncontrollable as the fright starts to shock the beat of my heart. The room spins as he takes a step towards me.

"No," I whine as I scramble across the floor.

My head is whipped back when his fist coils my long hair and I'm dragged across the room, my fingers clawing at the carpet as I try to get free from him.

"Please, God!" I cry through the tremble of my teeth. "NO!"

I'm flung onto the bed, and before I can escape, he's on me, his heavy body holding me hostage as his hands grapple with my wrists. I'm tied to the bed, the coarse rope he's using grazing my skin.

"Keep still," he growls as his hand covers my mouth.

My terrified eyes stare up at him as he starts to yank at his belt. I daren't move, not because of what he will do to me, but because I know the rampant tempo of my heart will surely push me into cardiac arrest should it shift into a higher gear.

He twists the belt around his hand until the leather strap presses against his palm, and the buckle swings freely from his tight hold. For the longest moment, neither of us moves, both of our eyes locking and saying so much, neither of us willing to break free from the other. The air shifts around me, the electric pulse in the air forcing every single hair on my body to stand on end as my blood shoots through my veins at a terrifying velocity.

Then, when the steel of his buckle connects with my face, the oxygen in the room seems to burst and I suck in a catastrophic amount of air, the effect causing my eyes to roll back when the pain registers.

He flips me over, the deep split in my cheek soaking the crisp white cotton of the pillow in a rush of crimson. My back arches when he brings his weapon back down, the metal tearing through the material of my tank top and rupturing my flesh so slickly that his black mask is sprayed with my blood. My flesh coats the walls as he brings down his belt time and time again, each of my screams fracturing the air.

"You fucking cunt of a whore!" he roars as his beating takes on a new level, each of his slashes now tearing into my spinal column as an overwhelming pain bursts out of me in a scream so fierce I can feel my throat rupture with the power of it.

"Nina!"

He's going to kill me. I know it deep within my bones. My mind accepts his punishing cruelty as my heartbeat slows. The blood is too much, and it's drowning me, swallowing me whole.

"Nina!"

Another scream is muted as blood drowns it out and my eyes droop. I don't have the energy to breathe anymore. I gurgle as the room fills with my blood, coating us both, staining my soul.

"NINA!"

My eyes snap open. Tricia is shaking me, her frantic cries breaking into my mind as her sobbing matches my own. I stare at her, my brain not registering what is happening until I feel the upsurge in my throat and vomit sprays everywhere.

"Jesus fucking Christ!" she screeches, horror on her face. "Fuck, Nina! Are you okay?"

I can't speak when my stomach reels off another round of sickness, my mouth unable to fully cope with the rush as it gushes from my nostrils.

"Fucking shit, Nina! I thought there was an intruder!

I thought I was going to die," Tricia cries as my bedroom door flies open and Devon barges in.

His eyes scan my bedroom as I stare in shock, his sudden entrance completely taking control of my mind and freeing me from the grip of my nightmare. His gaze finally lands on me and his eyes flow over me swiftly as if he's checking every part of me.

"Are you okay?" he asks, out of breath. "I heard screaming."

His chest is heaving, his face bright red. It's only then that I notice he's holding a gun.

"Oh my God!" I splutter.

He follows my stare to his hand then tucks the gun into the waistband of his pants. Walking across the carpet, he's by my side in seconds.

"Are you okay?" he asks again, his eyes narrow and heated as they burn a trail down my body.

"Yes," I whisper when my mouth dries further with his blatant perusal. I know he's checking for any injuries but I still shiver under his viewing, knowing that my nightwear shows all the silver and red scars that mark my body. "I had a nightmare."

His eyes widen. "Some nightmare. You woke up all the damn wildlife within a twelve mile radius. I thought someone was murdering you." He stumbles on the last few words as if pained by them, and scans the room to make sure it really was only a nightmare.

Embarrassment heats my cheeks and I lower my eyes. "I'm sorry. I didn't mean to wake you."

He shakes his head sternly. "Don't apologize. I'm just a little hyped up." He smiles sheepishly. "Hence the gun."

"Knight in shining armor, huh?" Tricia chuckles as we all start to relax.

He looks down at himself, dressed in only dress pants, and he smirks. "Well, I don't know about the armor."

"I agree, it's certainly penetrable, but you're definitely Nina's knight." She rests her hand on his shoulder . . . his bare shoulder. It's then that I fully realize his naked upper body, and the proximity of it. He's hard everywhere, each of his muscles defined. A shiver rakes my body and I snap my eyes back to his face as he stands.

"Well, if you ladies are sure you're okay, I'll get back to my own bed."

"Thank you," I whisper, my voice still locked down in the depths of my terror.

He stills and studies me, his brow plunging with his deep scrutiny. "Are you sure you're okay? You look very pale."

"I'm fine," I nod. "And once again, I apologize." I blow out a breath. "It's all I ever seem to do."

"Then stop. No need for apologies. We all have bad dreams."

"Just some more noisy than others," Tricia mumbles. Gaining a glare from Devon, she shrugs. "More terrifying than others, I mean." She looks at me with a deep question in her eyes.

I look away, lowering my eyes to the floor as I nod to both of them. "Goodnight, Devon. And thank you again."

"Sure," he murmurs, before he leaves as quickly as he came in.

Tricia is staring at me. I lick my lips and swallow. "I'm going to make coffee, then you, Nina Drake, are going to be honest with me once and for all."

She doesn't wait for my reply as she scuttles out of the room. I close my eyes and drag in a deep breath, my heart pounding with both what haunted my dreams and what is to haunt my talk with Tricia. But she has a right to know now. She's my best friend and if I can't open up to her, then who *can* I be honest with?

As I walk over to the window to pull the drapes back across, I catch Devon standing in his bedroom window, looking towards mine. For a moment we stare at each other, but then he steps close to his window and grasps the ledge, leaning his trim body towards me.

"I'm going to leave my window and drapes open, Nina. You ever need me then I'm there."

I don't reply. I can't. The emotion that surges through me takes my ability to vocalize any words. He smiles softly, then nods his head and walks away. It's strange, but I trust him. I can't understand or even begin to work out why; I just know he will stand by his promise.

"Thank you," I whisper into the night. I know he can't hear it, and once again, I sigh as I am grateful for someone else's help. Yet a part of me knows it's time to start accepting that I need help.

So turning, I brace myself and wait for Tricia.

Tricia stares at me, waiting, for what seems like forever. I can't look at her.

She slips her hand into mine and gives me an encouraging smile. "I know it's hard, Nee, but I think it would help if you opened up."

I nod.

"I know he raped you and he made a mess down there and everywhere," she continues, gesturing up and down my body. She really lacks subtlety. "But I think it's more than that."

I close my eyes, hating myself, but I swallow back my shame and whisper, "He made me come."

She stays quiet and I look at her, wondering what she doesn't have the nerve to say to my face but she's casually waiting for me to continue. She finally frowns at me and sucks in a breath. "What else?"

"Like that's not bad enough?" I stutter. "He made me come, Trish. He—made—my—own—body—turn—against—me! How sick am I?"

"Babe." She sighs, tightening her hand in mine. "Our minds don't control what arouses us. Fair enough, our eyes and our senses do, but if the erogenous zones on our body are stimulated, then they're stimulated. You shouldn't feel ashamed of that. It's natural." She wipes my tears away with her thumbs and sighs. "Please come home, Nee. The attack was forever ago."

I shake my head. "I can't."

"You can," she argues. "It's over. It's over."

"It will never be over, Tricia. Never."

"It was a year ago. Don't let him win. Don't allow him to rule your life even after his sickness took so much from you."

I look up at her through the torrent of my tears. "He's

coming back."

She freezes, her eyes narrowing as her throat lifts with a heavy gulp. "What?"

My skin prickles with the memory of his words, of his hatred. "He promised me that when I least expect him, he will come back. But the next time it will be to kill me."

She gasps and then blows it out. "Did he actually say those words? Did you tell the police that?"

"Yes. But they seem to think he was lying. They have his blood they found on the bedding from where I bit him, but they said they couldn't find a match on the system." Looking away I swallow the sob. "But I know he will come back, Trish. That's why I can't come back. I have to hide for the rest of my life."

"Oh, babe." She circles her arms around me and huddles me up.

Eighteen

Devon

I'M SO FUCKING ANGRY. WATCHING and listening to Nina makes my heart hurt. He promised me. He said she's mine now. I should have known better than to trust him. My own brother, and the spawn of my father.

The anger turns to rage and I swipe the contents from the old mahogany dresser in my bedroom, the many items crashing to the floor, glass and liquids coating the carpet in an explosion of anger.

I won't allow him to find her. He has no idea where I am, so I know as long as I'm careful, Nina will be safe.

My stomach twists with the knowledge that Noah made her come. But the only thought rushing through me is *'what if I can't?'* What if I can't make her come but Noah can? Then what? I hate how weak he's made me, how inadequate I'd felt under his scrutiny my entire life. I always saw him as an idol and felt that out of everyone in the world he actually cared and loved me, but the more I'm separated from him, the more I see with new eyes.

Watching her stroke herself off the other night was pure pleasure. Her beautiful face had turned into raw magnificence in the throes of her climax, her eyes squeezed shut and her mouth open as ecstasy overwhelmed her.

I hadn't been able to forget her in the twelve months she was away from me. She had taken something with her that day she left, some part of me that I needed to breathe. I hadn't understood what it was at first, and I was angry that she, a fucking bitch, had come between Noah and me. I hadn't understood it at all. Then after I dreamed of Courtney one night, I woke with a start, and a knowledge. A knowledge that I'm in love with Nina Drake.

Noah had seen it; that's why he had been so angry with me when I begged him not to hurt her. And I couldn't help but feel that, because of his anger with me, he had gone further than ever before. Not just tearing apart Nina's life, but the final piece of thread that held my family together.

But, and closing my eyes as I realize this, I miss the life I had with Noah. If I'm honest with myself, I haven't just lost my brother, I've lost a career that I loved. I miss the click of my camera, the life I captured in the lens, and each breath caught on film; breath that had been many women's last.

And I've started to imagine what she, Tricia, would look like in the click of death. I don't like the way she is with Nina; her mouth has no filter. She's reckless with her tongue, using it to shoot bullets that are having critical impact. She's too self-absorbed to even notice how incredibly broken her best friend is.

Nineteen

Nina

"I'M GOING TO MISS YOU," I sob to Tricia as I hug her tight to my body.

She pulls back, her own eyes full of tears, and nods. "Thank you for trusting me." She smiles. "I love you, babe. But please, please, put it behind you. Like I said, he won't be back for you. It was just his last way of hurting you."

I nod but she and I both know I don't believe her. "What will you do?"

I shrug as we both wave to Devon when he pulls off his driveway and disappears down the road. "I have no idea but I need to start trying to get a life back somehow.

I'm running out of money."

She frowns. "I can lend you a bit. I have some savings, but . . ."

I shake my head sternly. "No, don't be silly. I love you for offering but . . ." I blow out a breath. "Like you say, I need to move on, as hard as it might be."

"Well a job will hopefully give you the confidence you lost too. Then maybe one day soon you may make it home."

I grin at her, more tears running down my cheeks. I know she misses me. I miss her, and who knows, maybe she's right and one day I will make it home. But I'm not ready yet. Home isn't safe and still holds too many horrible memories.

Tricia looks towards Devon's house and gives me a sly smile. "Well, you're already making new friends."

"Friends, yes," I warn, knowing exactly where she's going. "Text me when you get home."

She chuckles but nods her head then hugs me tight again before she climbs into her car. A loud sob bursts from me and I wave like a lunatic as she pulls away and follows in Devon's wake, her car lights blinking at me as they turn around the corner.

I blink down at Steve when he curls himself around my legs, purring at me as though he senses my sadness. More likely that he's hungry. He's always hungry.

I scoop him up, nuzzling his soft fur as I carry him into the kitchen, my gaze towards the darkening sky. "There's a storm coming, big fella."

I'm apprehensive as the tree in the front yard sways towards the window with the force of the wind, its movement making the light from the streetlamp eerily chase across the walls of my dark lounge. Rain beats hard, the rattle of the glass pane causing me some concern. I pray that it holds against the sudden rainstorm that rolled in an hour ago. Summer storms are always the worst for me. The memories that come flooding in with them as destructive to my soul as they are to the surroundings.

The fire rages, and I pull the blanket higher up my body, snuggling down with my Kindle. It moves freely, and I blink at the bottom to where Steve is usually curled up.

"Steve?" I shout, looking around to see if he's curled up someplace new. But he isn't around. Frowning, I move off the sofa and check the house, my heart beat slowly increasing the more I hunt and can't find him. "Steve!"

Memories of a different storm flood in, and Ginger's wet coat is almost real in my mind. "STEVE!"

My eyes shift as quickly as my body as I carry my search upstairs. "Steve!" Freaking cat! "Where are you, baby?"

A clatter sounds as I enter my bedroom, causing me to jolt in terror. My body stiffens but I force myself to relax when I see the branches from the tree between mine and Devon's house crack the small window.

I peer out through the rain-contorted glass, my eyes

narrow as I hunt for my cat. I rush down the stairs and pull on my sneakers, then, grabbing my coat, I wrap it around me and venture out.

"STEVE?"

Where the hell is he? The trees are swaying fiercely with the force of the wind, the rain slashing me. My eyes search, my heart races, and still I see no sign of Steve. My legs can barely carry me with the dread burning through my body. Sweat pours from me, the saltiness teeming over my lips as the rain pushes it down my face.

Biting my lip, I brace myself and climb the few steps to my front porch, the image of a dead Ginger haunting me and making the shadows play cruel jokes as I imagine each silhouette is my poor, dead cat.

"Steve!" I choke out in a whisper as terror tightens my throat.

I knew he would be back; he told me. He told me and I didn't listen. I've been ignorant thinking he can't find me.

I run fast, around the house and through the back door, slamming it shut and housing each bolt in place as I snatch up my phone and call 911. It's an age before anyone answers my call, and as I'm about to slam the phone down and try again, a click notifies me of a connection.

As soon as the male voice answers me I'm already reeling off a string of slurred words.

"Ma'am, if you could calm down . . ."

"Calm down?" I bellow. "He's back! He's going to kill me. He's . . . he's got Steve . . . Steve is missing . . . he's going to hurt Steve . . ."

"Ma'am, who has Steve?"

"He does! He's going to kill him. He's coming for me.

Oh God, please help me. Please..."

"Okay, if you could calm down and tell me your name and where you are..."

I blurt out my name and address in between screeches of 'STEVE', my pounding heart disabling my words and making me have to repeat my address three times until the officer understands me.

"I'm afraid the sheriff's office is snowed under tonight, but I'll get someone round to you as fast as I can."

"He'll have killed him by then! You have to hurry. He's coming! He's coming for me."

"Ma'am, please. We'll be as quick as we can." Then the long lingering tone notifies me that once again, I'm alone. God damn small freaking villages with only one useless freaking cop. Why the hell did I move here? Then my mind tells me that wherever I am, he'll find me. And he'll kill me like he promised he would.

I scream when the lights go out, plunging me into darkness. The wind and rain hinders my hearing as I shuffle across the floor and into the cupboard under the stairs, frantically listening for footsteps. My heart is pounding so hard that all I can hear aside from the storm is my damn pulse.

"Calm down and concentrate, Nina!" I scold myself, desperately trying to cool the burn inside me, but the more I try and think, the more my mind shifts to the possibility that he's here, in my house once again.

My stomach aches for Steve. As much as he's a pathetic cat, he's still my family and I pray that *he* hasn't hurt him. Steve is the only living thing that really loves me and I need him, as insane as it sounds. He's my comfort blanket, my listening ear when I'm stressed. His huge grey eyes look at me as though he's listening whenever I'm in a mood, either sobbing, or ranting about life.

I don't know how long I'm hidden under the stairs before my whole body tenses and my ears finally catch a noise. My throat hurts so much that I daren't swallow the moisture suddenly coating my mouth. I beg my heart to stop beating, its frantic rhythm loud in the solitude of my hiding place.

The faint squeal is the front door opening, and I hate myself when I start to weep. I can't do this again. I won't survive it again.

Footsteps thump across the floor and I huddle further back into the closet, praying to God for the first time in my life as I try desperately to hold my breath.

"Hello!" a man shouts. I frown. Would he actually call out? To him this would be a game, of hide and seek, life and death, and I'm sure he wouldn't allow me any inkling of where he is. "Hello, Ma'am? It's Sheriff Logan. You called in an emergency."

I blow out a breath, my heart threating to tear through my breastbone in relief. Creaking open the door slightly, a flash of light illuminates the wall above my head from the sheriff's flashlight. He peers down at me when I poke my head out and smiles. "Nina Drake?"

I nod, whimpering as I scramble out. "Oh, thank God."

"I'm so sorry it took me a while. The girl who mans the phones went into labor tonight, left me and my sergeant on our own, and of course it has to be the busiest night of the year," he rambles, with a huge welcoming smile. Sensing my panic, he studies me and straightens his shoulders.

"You dialed 911 about someone entering your premises and your friend being kidnapped and hurt."

I frown. "My friend is okay."

Pulling out a small flipbook, he points his light at it and squints at the page then looks back at me. "Steve?"

"Oh." I shake my head. "Steve isn't my friend, he's my cat."

I want to recoil when he stiffens and stares at me in bewilderment. "You called 911 because your cat is missing?" His shock is as clear, as his disgust with me, but I shake my head.

"You don't understand."

"Then would you care to explain?" His lip curls slightly as his eyes trace down my body with his torchlight. I tell myself that he's checking for injuries, not actually checking me out. When I'm unable to get the horror of my past out, he blinks at me, the contempt he shows offering me no solace.

"Ma'am? Would you care to tell me why you called an emergency service for a missing cat when I have extremely important calls to answer?" He steps towards me. "Calls that are real emergencies."

I stare at him, my mouth open like a goddam fish but still my nerves allow nothing out.

"MA'AM?"

I jump back, his anger forcing more tears to slide down my face. "He . . . assaulted me . . . he's coming . . ." It's all I can manage, my voice quiet with both shame and terror.

He frowns at me, his head tilting to the side as his expression softens. It's obvious he's seen my fear. Reaching out, his fingers curl softly around my arm. "Please, come and sit down." Directing me slowly across the path of his light, he leads me to the sofa. "The lights are out within a forty kilometer vicinity," he explains as he perches on the sofa beside me and lays his light on the table so the beam is directed towards us. "Damn storm."

I stare at the fire, my heart rate a little slower, but my senses are hyper-alert, my eyes still skimming over every inch of the room.

"Would you like to tell me what's going on?" Sheriff Logan presses softly.

I can't seem to control my own body, and I sit there, mute and numb. Swallowing back the bile I try and explain, with as little detail as possible.

"My cat . . . my old cat. He was . . . killed."

The sheriff nods but his face doesn't express what he's thinking, which is probably that he thinks Ginger was run over, or poisoned by a farmer with a grudge.

Keeping my gaze on the flames of the fire, I squeeze my eyes closed. "His killer attacked me. He . . . he raped me and . . . hurt me. And he promised that he would be back."

The sheriff nods and squeezes my arm soothingly. "Okay, Nina."

Finally I lift my eyes and look at him. He's smiling at me reassuringly, his eyes as soft as his expression. "I'm going to take a look around for you, check everything out, and then we can decide what to do about your cat . . . Steve."

I nod and manage a grateful smile, swiping at the tears burning my cheeks. "Thank you."

Nodding again, he takes off into the hallway, his flashlight bouncing off every surface as he leaves me with only the light of the fire. I close my eyes. I tell myself it's not a perfect opportunity for my stalker to grab me, or hit the sheriff over the head then tie him up and make him witness another rape. I scold myself when my mind taunts me with cruel images of Steve swinging on the porch, his neck sliced open and his blood redecorating the clean wooden decking.

I jolt when the sheriff enters. "Everything is clear, Ma'am. There's no one here."

I blow out a breath of pure relief and my eyes pop wide when I hear a soft meow. Both the Sheriff and I look down when Steve crawls out from under the sofa, stretching his long body as he purrs his hello.

Heat flames my face and I cringe. "Oh good God. Now I really do look like a paranoid nutjob."

The sheriff chuckles and shakes his head. "Don't worry about it. Believe me, we get worse."

Steve jumps onto my lap and Sheriff Logan reaches down and strokes his head. "Well, everything appears to be in order." His cell phone rings from his pocket and he grimaces as he pulls it out. "Sorry. Disadvantage of having your only switchboard operator off having a baby. You'd think she'd be more considerate." He winks as he answers his phone.

It's obviously another emergency, a real one this time, as he nods and thrusts a card at me. Covering the mouthpiece of the phone, he smiles as he heads for the door. "Any more problems, that number directs you straight to my cell. No matter how paranoid you think you're being, or if you lose Steve to a warm spot under any furniture, you call me. And Nina . . ."

I look into his compassionate blue eyes. "Yes?"

"I won't let anyone come into my town and hurt a resident, you hear me?"

I smile widely and nod. "Thank you."

"Just my job, honey. Protect and serve and all that jazz." He rubs my shoulder. Huh, I didn't shudder. Perhaps I will be safe here.

Then he's gone, leaving me glaring at a blasé, in extreme trouble, Steve. As if sensing my anger, he turns his back on me, whips up his tail, and saunters off. Then the lights flick back on and I flop back down on the sofa and realize my life needs to take a drastic turn before I end up killed by my own paranoia.

Twenty

It's a warm Monday the day after the storm, the hottest of the year so far, and I've decided to tackle the garden. It's shamefully overgrown, and every time I sneak a look to Devon's, the more mine seems to resemble a jungle.

Steve, 'The Sun God', is baking under the intense rays, his large round tummy facing the sky as he proudly shows off his assets to the birds that mock him from one of the trees.

"You're such a rude boy!" I chastise.

He turns his face to me, the sound of my voice grabbing his attention. His tongue peeks out and he decides it's the perfect time to wash his bits and pieces.

Holding up my hands, I roll my eyes. "I rest my case.

Why don't you trim off that tum and go chase some mice like normal cats do?"

He stills, one of his eyes larger than the other as he regards me with disgust.

"No," I continue as I pull at a few weeds embedded deeply into the tough soil that is soaked through from the storm last night. "Why should you when you have a mommy that brings you all you like to eat in the convenience of pouches, gravy included, no cooking to do and no dishes?" I chuckle, grimacing at a worm that pops its head through the earth to see what the noise is all about. "I should call you Sir Steve. It suits you."

He gets up and saunters down the garden, his tiny little puckered hole directed at me. I'm sure it's his personal way of flipping me off.

"Well, that told you." Devon laughs from his garden.

I look over, not realizing I'd had an audience, but smile. "I'm sure in a previous life that darn cat was waited on hand and foot."

He laughs as he rests his backside on the low wall between our houses. "I see you're getting to grips with nature." I look down and study the six inch plot I've managed to clear and smile proudly. "Although the *weed* you just pulled up was actually white clover."

My mouth pops open and I look to the *weed* laid on its side with the other *weeds*. "Oops. I told you I'm rubbish at this."

He gives me a warm smile. "Why don't you let me have a go at it this week?"

"Oh, I can't ask you to do that!"

"You haven't asked me, I've offered. Besides, it's something I love to do so it's not exactly a great chore."

"Okay." I smile, picking myself up from the grass and wiping the dirt off my jeans. "Thank you. I'm just about to grab a cold beer. Would you like one?" My heart beats frantically when I hope he doesn't misinterpret my offer as something more but he nods before I can worry further.

"That sounds good. This heat is unreal."

"Isn't it?" I say over my shoulder when he climbs over the wall and follows me into the kitchen.

"So how long have you lived round here?" he asks, smiling in thanks as he takes the bottle from me.

"About a year."

"And there's no one else . . ." he looks around my kitchen, " . . . in your life?"

My mouth dries a little. I'm scared to say it's only me, just in case he takes it as an offer for more than a friendship but then I scold myself. Why do I always think the worst of people? "No, there's just me . . . and Steve."

He nods then takes a gulp of his beer and I can't help but watch the movement of his Adam's apple as the liquid pours down his throat.

"And there's no one in your life?" I ask as casually as possible. He shakes his head, his eyes regarding me questioningly. I smile. "I wasn't sure if the guy who helped you move in was your boyfriend."

He chokes on his drink. "Chris? No, he's just a friend."

Quiet descends as we both take sips from our bottles, our eyes on one another. I can't tell if he's checking me out or if he's just being friendly. He seems very 'real', his eyes forthcoming all of his thoughts but then he smiles.

"Have you had any particular thoughts about the garden?"

Shaking my head, I let my gaze roam out of the window and into the wilderness that seems to go on for miles. "If I'm honest, I find the size of it a bit daunting. I don't know where to start."

"Well, if we clear the top part first, I can fix you up a line for your laundry. And then when the bottom is sorted I can move it down there out of the way. That way you don't have your undies flapping in your face while you're trying to catch the rays."

I laugh at the image in my head. "That sounds good. Thank you."

He drains his bottle and nods. "Right I'll make a start."

I stare at him in amusement. "Wow, you're eager."

He chuckles then pats his stomach. "I have to keep this in shape somehow, and with no job prospects for a while, working in the garden keeps me sane."

I nod, knowing exactly how he feels. I realize how hard it must be for him to find work out here. It isn't exactly a thriving industrial town so the choice of work available is scarce. "Yeah, I know."

Blinking at me, he smiles in understanding then seems to shake himself and salutes me. "All I ask is that you keep the liquid flowing."

I straighten my shoulders and nod firmly. "Consider it done, Boss."

He chuckles and rolls his eyes then makes his way out. I hate the pull in my stomach when my eyes drop to his rear. What the hell is wrong with me? Nothing for a year then I suddenly turn into a crazy sex-starved woman who keeps ogling her damn neighbor.

Shaking off my thoughts, I get cracking with my first job—uncapping another beer.

Three weeks later both Devon and I are grinning at the beauty of my new yard. It's huge. Devon chopped back hedge after hedge and revealed yet more garden beyond the realms of what we thought possible.

Where before had been brambles, weeds and long grass, now accommodates a large grassed area with pretty border flowers. At the far end, Devon paved slabs and erected a washing line, and I smile as I watched my bed sheets blowing briskly in the wind.

"I don't know what to say, Devon."

"You don't have to say anything. I've enjoyed it. I'm amazed at the rare plants I found."

I quirk a brow and nudge him with my elbow as we sit on the top step of the decking at the rear of the house, "Don't tell me, you uprooted them and they're currently under bid on eBay!"

His eyes widen in shock but then he laughs, his head tipping back with his hearty guffaw. "Is that Sass Misses?" He smirks at me then motions for me to follow him over to the wall between our houses. I follow his gaze and peek over.

Spinning around I slap his arm playfully. "You stole my plants!"

He laughs at my shock. "Actually I just took a cutting.

We both have rare plants now."

Shaking my head I can't help but laugh. "Okay, I'll let you off. Anyway," I say as we both walk back towards the chairs we previously occupied, "I've made a decision." He lifts his brow, gesturing for me to go on but doesn't say anything. "I'm going to apply for a job at the Sheriff's office."

Both his eyebrows lift. I'd come to the decision whilst in bed last night. Over the past few weeks, working with Devon in the garden, I've been the happiest I've been in a long time. Apart from his company, which I thoroughly enjoy, I realized it's because I had a purpose to get up in a morning. The hard work stopped the incessant daily torment in my mind and I figured it's about time I move forward.

"Well, that's great." He seems genuinely happy for me, and hesitantly, I reach over and place my hand over his.

"I want to thank you, really. It's been these past few weeks in the garden, with you, that's made me realize I need something more out of life, other than Steve, of course," I add when the big grey ball of fluff comes sauntering up the garden without a care in the world, with a field mouse trapped between his jaws.

"What the hell, Steve!" I squeal and skip across the decking when he drops it at my feet.

Devon laughs loudly as he fetches the small trowel from where he'd left it beside the flower bed, and scoops up the horrible little thing. "He's just bringing you a gift!"

"Well he can take his 'gift' and bury it with the rest of his shit in the gravel."

He gawps at me. "You cussed!"

My own eyes widen and I shake my head at Steve. "You're such a bad influence."

"Well, actually." Devon chuckles. "You can't blame Steve. He can't talk so you haven't learned it from him."

I glare at him and point a finger to his chest. "Then I blame you!"

He nods and sighs. "Of course."

Smiling, I nudge him again. "Come on, I'll treat us to a greasy burger and fries."

He stares at me, his brow a little furrowed. "Are we actually going out?"

I stiffen and swallow. Could I do that? Go out to eat? "No, I'll order in."

Looking like he is disappointed his eyes drop and those darn teeth make an appearance, biting down on his plump bottom lip as he nods his head. "Okay, but I want the biggest burger on the menu."

Giving him a smug smile, I lick my lips, "And because I've *worked* so hard in my garden, I think I'll join you."

His mouth pops open but he shakes his head and laughs. "You should get the biggest there is. After all those calories you've burnt *gardening* you need to stock up."

I nod, ignoring his sarcasm as I stroll into the house. "This figure doesn't get like this on its own, you know? It needs all the help it can get." I know he's staring at my backside as I walk away, and for the first time in a long time, I don't care.

How's that for progress?

Twenty-One

I BLOW OUT A BREATH as I stare at the front window of the sheriff's office. I know I don't know what I'm doing but I need to do this. Heather encouraged it; she seems to think I'm ready. Me? Well, I'm not so sure, but gritting my teeth and pulling my shoulders straight, I step inside.

It's a large room, old and dusty with one desk facing the door and another three towards the back. Various flyers are stuck to the walls and the place smells like week old pizza.

A round, middle-aged man in a cop uniform rises from his desk near the rear of the room and strolls towards me with a wide toothy grin. "Good morning, Miss."

I give him a smile although my eyes are still hunting

the room. "Umm, is Sheriff Logan in?"

He nods then bellows at the top of his voice. "Luke! Lady at the front desk for you!"

A door I hadn't noticed to the left of the room opens and the sheriff pops his head round. "Two minutes."

The sergeant looks at me and opens his mouth but I smile and hold up a hand. "I heard. Thank you."

I'm amazed by the lack of space, but then again, the coziness of it is quite pleasant. The police department in the city is huge, its many floors very daunting and formal, but this small office is really quaint, Sheriff Logan smiles as he walks towards me, his mouth around a sandwich.

"I'm so sorry. I'm disturbing your lunch."

Shaking his head, he waves off my apology. "It's not a problem. We're used to working and eating here."

"Ain't that the truth," the sergeant scoffs around his own snack when the phone rings on his desk. "Just one day!" he grumbles as he throws down his burger. "One damn day would be nice."

Sheriff Logan rolls his eyes but smiles. "How can I help you, Nina?"

"Oh, you remember me?" I'm surprised but then I remember the way I handled the situation with 'missing' Steve and my face flushes with embarrassment.

"Of course," he says simply, his eyes not showing any amusement or mockery. "You'll find that in small towns like this, we get to know everyone."

"Yes, I suppose so." I nod in agreement. "Anyway," I blurt out quickly before I lose my nerve and back out. "Ummm, you mentioned that your receptionist has had a baby and left your office unmanned." He nods, encour-

128

aging me to go on. His blue eyes are large but they twinkle kindly, his long, dark lashes fluttering every time he blinks. He seems to have a way about him that sets me at ease, and although he appears to be in his early thirties he gives the impression of a knowledgeable man. I can't quite seem to work it out but I sense his friendliness, especially when he smiles. "Well, I was wondering if you were looking for a fill in while she's out of action."

His eyes widen on me but his face breaks into a huge grin. "Are you serious?"

I nod, swallowing back my anxiety. The local bar is advertising for a bartender, and one of the shops in town wants a shelf stacker, but the way I figure it, there's no place safer to work than in the local police department.

"Do you have any law degrees?"

My mouth drops open. Of course I would need some kind of degree or training.

He holds his hands up and laughs. "I'm teasing you, sweetheart." I hope the blush I feel isn't as prudent as I imagine. "The pay won't be great," he mumbles with a grimace but I shake my head and smile.

"That's fine." I'm not going to tell him I only want the job to toughen myself up. That is worth more than any amount.

Sheriff Logan turns and looks at his sergeant who has the biggest grin on his face. "Gerry?"

"Hell yes." The man laughs as the phone starts to ring once again.

"Then you have yourself a job." The sheriff grins and gestures to the seat behind the desk with the wave of a hand.

"You want me to start now, Sheriff?"

"Please, call me Luke, and there's no time like the present, Nina."

I stare at him for a moment before I shrug and walk around the desk, a little bewildered by how easy it is. "Okay then. You'd better show me the ropes."

Over the next few weeks, Luke showed me everything the job included, introduced me to the other cop who works there, Brady, and I took to it as easily as I did when I first attended bar. *Not one broken mug*

In fact I would even go as far as saying, I love it. I've found something I'm good at, along with gaining back a small piece of life outside the four walls of my house. Steve doesn't like it, though. He misses me, and for the previous three days I arrived home after a long day, he's ignored me, refusing to eat his food and giving me the cold shoulder. It saddens me because, in a stupid way, apart from Tricia, he's my best friend.

Tricia is delighted by my news, especially the part about the 'single' sheriff, as is Heather, only she's proud of my determination to put the last twelve months behind me, and secretly, I'm proud of myself too.

It took too long for me to finally accept that I was letting him win. This was exactly what he wants, me hiding from life. It was another way to hurt me and foolishly, I had allowed him to manipulate me, even though he's no longer in my life.

It is my life, and although I'm not ready to go out clubbing or join the local church group, it's a start. And we all have to start somewhere.

Twenty-Two

Devon

It's early, and I watch Nina skip down her porch steps from my bedroom window, her long hair swaying as if it's as happy as she is. She's started to trade her customary jeans and tee for classy pants and blouses. She's even begun to wear a smidgen of lipstick and mascara, and her beauty has tripled with her happiness.

I smile to myself. It's nice to see her finally putting Noah's monstrous act behind her. Not only does it mean she's finally moving on, but she's also more likely to let me in. And I crave that more than air. The last few weeks spent with her in her yard have been the best. And although there have been a few intense moments where it seems like we're getting closer, I'm content with her friendship. I hadn't realized how lonely my life had been until I spent time with Nina. It saddens me as my thoughts regularly move to Noah and how much I really do miss him.

I missed her return yesterday. Being bored out of my skull now that Nina's job is thwarting my watch over her, I ended up at the pub in town. I can't even remember getting home due to the sheer volume of whisky I consumed. I don't do it often enough. Although I'd sat in a corner completely on my own, the peace in my mind amazed me. I'd people watched, played a game with myself as to what each resident did with their lives. And I'd pictured Nina and I, us a couple, both of us playing the game.

Another smile lifts my lips at the thought, and I make my way down the stairs. I'm happy this morning, and pleased I'm not suffering from a hangover.

I roll my eyes with amusement when I catch Steve climbing through the window in the hallway. He looks up at me and gives me a quiet meow in greeting.

"Mommy left you again?" Steve has been coming to me for days, his visits coinciding with Nina's work hours. He was used to the full daytime attention from her, and now that she's going out he's struggling with the isolation, so he visits me and we've formed a strange friendship.

My breath catches in my throat when I walk into the kitchen. My eyes furiously scan my surroundings as my nose catches a tell-tale fishy smell. Steve, oblivious to the offending item, jumps onto the table and sticks his nose in the open pizza box, his small tongue lapping at the tuna and cheese pizza. I hate tuna. *Noah loves it.*

My throat aches as I stand frozen and mute in the middle of the room. He's been here. He must have. There is no way I would buy that shit. My teeth crack under the pressure when my jaw clenches.

I swat Steve out of the way, unlock the back door, and

throw the disgusting pizza in the trash, my gaze roaming the garden to find anything out of place. But other than the pizza, there's nothing.

I blink, trying to get my mind to work through last night's activities but I can't remember much after the sixth whiskey.

"Shit!"

This is bad news, especially now Nina is moving on. I want to warn her but I know it'll put her back again and compromise the friendship we've established. Yet I also know that, whether warned or not, if Noah wants her, then he'll get to her.

My hands shake as I pour coffee, my heart pounding in rhythm with the vibrations in my body as I lower myself into a chair and fire up the laptop.

Steve is wrapping himself around my legs, his purr loud in the quiet. I know he wants food but I'm too shaken up to get back up, my legs like jelly and my hands unable to hold my mug.

A ping at the laptop catches my attention and I look down. My stomach vaults up my throat, last night's alcohol making a swift return when the email pops up in the top right-hand corner.

TO: Devon2035
FROM: NOAH

Hello brother. Nice house.
. . . and a very pretty neighbor.

Twenty-Three

Nina

"Point Rose town Sheriff's department," I sing down the phone when I answer the first call of the afternoon.

I roll my eyes when Mrs. Perry's gravelly voice slurs through the earpiece. Even though I've only been working here a few weeks, I'm already familiar with Mrs. Perry and her paranoia. I thought I was bad but this woman makes me seem like a normal, sane individual. "Nina? Is that you, dear?"

"It is, Mrs. Perry. Good afternoon. What can I do for you today?"

"Richie's been again. He's taken some beans and my

favorite candy."

I stifle the groan and try to sound polite. "Mrs. Perry, I urge you again to take the key from Richie. There's really nothing we can do if you keep allowing your son access to your home."

"But he stole from me. I can't afford to replace the items."

"I shall make sure the items are returned Mrs. Perry," I promise, making a note to call into the store and pick up the darn items myself.

I catch Luke smirking at me as he passes the front desk, his characteristic amused grin making me chuckle to myself. He mimics playing a violin and I reach over and slap him, giving him a mock glare. He laughs and disappears into his office.

"Oh, so you're going to send an officer here?"

I debate sending Luke to her house, just for payback, but even I'm not that cruel. "I'm sorry but all the officers are out dealing with emergencies. But don't worry, I'll make sure the goods are returned today." I end the call before she can argue with me and shake my head.

Gerry quirks a brow at me. "Had enough yet?"

I laugh. "She's just old and lonely."

He scoffs. "Are you surprised she's lonely? The woman makes Annie Wilkes look normal." *'And me'* comes to mind but I shake my head at him.

"You read *Misery*?" I question with a suspicious undertone.

"I read," he says, but I keep a raised brow and a narrowed eye on him until he breaks. "Fine. I saw the movie. Who has time to read these days?"

"Smart people," I counter in jest.

"Is it lunch time yet?" Luke shouts from his office.

Brady, Logan's deputy and department skirt chaser—according to Gerry, checks his watch and nods. "Right on time." Both Gerry and I look at the large clock on the wall and as Brady stated, Luke is right on time. He is more reliable than an alarm clock where food is concerned.

I smile and pick up my purse. "Usual?" I shout back. He looks up from his desk and grins at me through the window.

"Where have you been all my life?" he asks as he places his hand over his heart.

"Avoiding you!" Gerry says as I make my way out.

Betty looks up and smiles when she sees me enter her teashop. "Hey, Nina. The usual?"

I nod. "Of course, although I think I'll have just a scone. My stomach seems a little tender today."

Her face falls and she looks at me with concern. "Oh, I do hope you're not coming down with something."

"Mmm, me too."

"Would you like butter, dear?"

I nod and smile. "Please," I mumble, picking up a flyer as she turns back into the kitchen. It's advertising the town festival coming next weekend. My mouth dries. I'd love to go but the crowds and noise might be a bit too much.

"We can go together if you want," a voice whispers over my shoulder.

I spin around and smile at Devon. "Hello."

His smile is huge, his eyes lighting as he regards me. "Do you want to?" I frown at him in confusion. "The festival. If it's a bit too much for you on your own, I would be more than happy to go with you. We're both new here so it would probably be a good idea." He leans forwards and rests his mouth at my ear. "I'll protect you from the crazy village people."

I can't help but chuckle, even though a throb hits my belly with his closeness. His warm breath on my neck causes a shiver to ripple down my spine. I'm almost panting when I look up at him. His expression has softened and his smile has disappeared, giving him an intense look. My mouth dries as I stare up at him, his eyes boring into me as if he's experiencing the same tingling sensation.

"Would you like jelly on your scone?" Betty shouts from the back of the store, making me blink and step back.

"Umm, yes." I shout back. "Yes, please."

"So?" Devon asks, and I blink.

"Sorry, what?"

He laughs loudly and shakes his head. "The festival, Nina. Do you want to go?"

"Oh." I glance back down to the flyer in my hand, the stalls and entertainment promised making me long to go, so once again forcing my courage, I nod. "Yeah, why not?"

He grins. "It's a date."

My eyes widen in shock but he's gone. That was the last thing I meant. He's my neighbor, my friend. I hope he doesn't think there's something more in it for him. I admit there's something about Devon that makes my body aware for the first time in so long, but I can't act on it. The thought of having an intimate relationship again makes my stomach heave, and the repulsive scars that decorate nearly every inch of my skin would surely douse any desire he has for me.

I can't help but let my gaze fall to his backside as he walks towards his car across the street, right outside the office. I hadn't even seen it. So much for my vigilance.

Twenty-Four

Devon

I FLING MY KEYS IN the bowl on the dresser by the front door. I can't stop grinning. I'm already thinking about what I should wear to the festival. Jeans and a smart tee? Dress pants and a shirt? Jeans and a dress shirt? Damn, I'm acting like a woman, but this is progress for both of us. She'd shut herself away from the world, and little does she know, I've lived my whole life doing the same.

Steve purrs up at me, greeting me into my own home. "Hey, buddy." I scoop him up and carry him to the kitchen, placing him and my groceries onto the counter before pulling out a can of his favorite salmon. "Got you a treat today."

He nuzzles me. I like that we've become friends. I dig out a portion of fish onto his saucer, and he dives in hungrily. I must remember to tell Nina of my frequent visitor; she'll be wondering why his stomach is getting bigger.

I grab a can of soda, walk into the lounge, and sink onto the sofa. I frown when I place my soda down and see the TV remote control on the coffee table. I'm sure I put it back in its place before I went out last night. It's then that I notice the television on standby, the orange flashing light telling of my absentmindedness.

I don't know why or what makes me press the power button, but when I do and the paused image springs to life, I can't seem to take a breath.

I watch with wide eyes the sway of her long dark hair as she hangs from the chain, her slim body covered in blood and filth. She's unconscious, her naked body swaying in the still of the bare room. I can't drag my eyes away from the horrific scene. My fingers twitch and I hate the emptiness in my hand. I miss my camera but I hate that I miss it more. There are no shadows and no other items in the dimly lit room, but I know he's there, taunting me from behind his own camera.

Coming back to my senses, I stab at the stop button and fall to my knees before the DVD player, hitting eject multiple times before I aim right and it spews out the disc. It's a plain disc with no writing on it, only the manufacturer's mark. Pressing my fingers into it until my knuckles turn white, I snap it in half.

"Stop it!" I blurt out to the empty room. "Just stop!" I spring to my feet, turning in circles as I look at every corner, hunting for cameras. "Why won't you leave me be? Let me move on?"

Rushing into the kitchen, disturbing Steve who is cleaning his paws, I force the offending disc into the trash and slam down the lid. Then grabbing the lid again, I pull some rubbish from the bottom of the can and bring it to the top, burying the disc in the middle.

My head is throbbing as hard as my heart. I'm sweating, the drops sliding down my forehead and leaking into my eyes.

What the fuck does he want? He took what he could from Nina, why does he want more?

"WHY?" I yell, sending Steve scuttling out, then falling to my knees. "Please. Please . . ."

But he's not listening. I know he's not. Even if he hears me, he's not listening. And I know he won't stop until he's ruined me. And Nina Drake.

I punch my fist through the glass pane of the back door and wince from the abrasion, leaking blood on to the floor. "Damn it."

Running my hand under the tap, I clean up the cut the best I can but the bleeding won't stop and I know I need stitches. Perfect.

The nearest hospital is twenty miles away, but the town has a medic that should be qualified to handle a few stitches. I drive there using my one good hand, the blood now decorating my jeans. I look like someone tried to shoot my junk off. What a foolish thing to do.

The receptionist gasps at my dramatic entry; luckily the waiting area is empty. Got to love small towns.

"Any chance I can see the doc?"

She flusters, picking up the phone and pressing a red button. The door to the far left of the small space opens, and a middle-aged woman wearing casual clothes with a white doctor's coat over them pokes her head out. She rushes over to me and hurries me into her office with a hand pushing firmly on my lower back. "What happened to you . . . ? Forgive me, I don't know your name."

"Devon Trent."

"New in town?" She takes my hand in hers and unwraps the tea towel I'd used as a Band-Aid to cover the weeping gash.

"Yes. I moved in not too long ago."

"You need to go to the hospital." She swipes over my hand, avoiding the two inches wide incision that's at least a half an inch deep.

"Can't you fix it up?"

"I can, but I shouldn't. You need to go to the hospital. Do you have health insurance?"

No. Noah always felt we were safer keeping ourselves out of any data systems. In fact, this is the first time in my life I can remember ever setting foot in a doctor's office.

"I'll pay cash," I say.

Her eyes travel up to meet mine, a slight question in her eyes, but she shrugs it off. "Are you allergic to anything?"

My brows crash together when I say, "I don't know."

She pauses from cleaning my wound, her penetrating gaze making me feel vulnerable and uneasy all at once. "Okay, well I'll take some samples to make sure it isn't infected, and add you to my patient list. I will have to stitch this without local anesthetic, just in case you have a reaction."

"Just do what you have to do, doc, and thank you."

Twenty-Five

Nina

"Nina, can you come in here quickly before you leave?"

I ignore Gerry's tuts, mocking me as if I'm being called into the boss' office for a disciplinary. It's almost six o clock. The day has been a long one, and soon the office will be occupied with the two night shift officers who resemble security guards at the mall more than policemen. Fortunately, things are quiet around here at night and Luke keeps his phone on in case of emergencies.

I poke my head into his office and he waves me in to sit down opposite him.

"Now, I know this is sensitive and I don't want you to

get the wrong idea and think I'm snooping, but it's my job to follow up on any call made to the department, especially when I follow it up with a house call." I shift in my seat, lowering my face. "Also, with you working for the department, I had to do a background check." He leans forward and shuffles some paperwork.

"What did it say?" I whisper, chancing a quick look up at him and wishing I hadn't when I see pity, anger and something else I can't decipher in his eyes.

"It has the medical file with the list of injuries you sustained during a four hour assault." Bile thickens in the back of my throat. "It has the police report that's still ongoing."

My hand reaches up to rub at the scars on my chest that are throbbing in my mind. "They didn't catch him," I murmur. "They don't even have a suspect."

He stiffens and grinds his teeth, his jaw clenching for a moment. "Tell me about the bar owner, Todd."

I inhale and look up into his blue eyes that are focused on my hand rubbing at the scars. I pull the file from under his hand and open it before he can stop me. Photographs taken by the nurse glare at me as if mocking me, their close-up view making the bile that twists my stomach mutate into vomit.

"Nina, don't," he warns but it's too late. I need to see them. Angry red welts lap over each other on my back from the belt he took to me, the white bed sheet beneath me stained crimson. Holes, bloody and raw from his teeth scatter my chest. I remember one of the nurses breaking down into a heap on the floor, sobbing, unable to cope with what she was witnessing. She was reprimanded and sent out of the room. Black, swollen eyes, unrecognizable to my own vision. Lumps and patches void of hair from him ripping clumps out are all visible under the scrutiny of the cameras flash.

My breathing becomes labored as I move through photo after photo. A sob rips from my chest when a specific picture showing between my thighs during the rape examination comes into view. So much bruising and swelling it doesn't even look like part of a human being. He destroyed me. How could someone be this evil? Who raised him to be such a debauched version of mankind? Why did he hate me so much? It felt personal. He tortured me. *What's more personal than that?*

I throw the photos back into the file and sling it back on his desk. I can't look at them anymore. I'm finally getting my life back on track. I don't need those reminders; my own nightmares are enough.

"Todd had an alibi and he wasn't the right height or weight anyway. Look Luke, I'm tired and . . ."

"What about the neighbor, a Mr . . . ?"

I laugh. "Mr. Ilavich? He's too old and I would have recognized his voice. The assailant was strong, tall . . . and evil," I finish on a choked whisper.

He flicks through the file, huffing every now and again, and I flinch knowing he has seen my most intimate parts.

"But Mr. Ilavich moved a couple of weeks after the assault and hasn't been located since."

I shiver in response. "Really?"

He hands me the folder showing my old house, and his, boarded up with 'For Sale' signs pushed into the dry dirt out front.

"Was there ever anything *off* about him?"

I laugh again but the humor is absent this time. "He was a little creepy. He was kind of . . . a perv, for lack of a better explanation." I shrug.

"Did he ever try anything with you or come across aggressive?"

I shake my head. "I caught him with a young girl that looked a lot like me once doing . . ." A blush creeps over my skin at the thought of it.

"Doing?"

I scrunch my nose. "Oral?" I pose it as a question but I don't mean to, I'm embarrassed, and anything sexual intimidates me now.

"Okay, well, I'm going to try and track this guy down."

I stand up, moving closer to the desk separating us. "Do you really think he had something to do with it?" Why would he want someone to hurt me like that? He always appeared to favor me. I fed his damn dog!

"It doesn't hurt to ask questions and eliminate people. Now get yourself home, and, Nina . . ." I look right into his worried eyes. "If you remember anything or you just want to talk, you have my number. Use it anytime." I thank him then make my way home not even stopping to pick up dinner.

My stomach growls when I push my key into the front door, and I'm greeted with no cat, and no food to eat. I really must make a better effort to pick up groceries. I know I'm out of cat food, and while I'd starve for the night, Steve will not and he'll whine and meow all night until I'm forced to get up and feed him something. Picking my car keys back up, I sigh, feeling tired and defeated.

I make it to my car and squint when Devon's full beams blast me in the eyes. He pulls onto his drive, the gravel crunching under the pressure of his tires. I wait to say hello so he doesn't think I'm being rude, not saying hello.

He takes his time maneuvering his large frame from the small seat. Straight away, the aroma of pizza wafts through the air and hits me straight in the face. My stomach grumbles loudly, eliciting a chuckle from Devon.

"Hungry?" He smirks and it's cute; it reaches his eyes.

"Long day. I forgot to grab dinner." I shrug and open my car door.

"Hey, you can share mine. I won't eat all this by myself anyway."

I doubt that's true. I could easily down half of that in my starving state right now and I'm half the size of him. It's then that I notice a bandage wrapped around his palm. "What happened?" I slam my car door shut and wander over to him, taking the bag that has a bottle of liquor inside from the hand in question. He looks sheepish and nods over to the back door that leads out of the side of his house, directly opposite my own. One of the small square panes of glass is smashed.

"Accident. I'm clumsy and heavy-handed. Come inside and eat with me... please?" He offers with such a plea that it's hard to resist. He must be lonely too. I haven't seen his friend here since the day he moved in, and no visitors have ever been here when I've been home.

"As tempting as that pizza smells, I need cat food or Steve will abandon me for a better hostess." I roll my eyes.

"I fed Steve earlier."

"You did?" My tone is a little harsher than I intend, the hectic day and draining conversation with Luke taking its toll.

"He kind of lets himself in any open window. I didn't mean to offend you by keeping some food in the house for him. He keeps me company from time to time." He winces and I feel like a jackass for being a bitch over a cat that isn't even mine in the first place. He came to me the same way, and I adopted him without permission or seeking out any previous owner. I'm being selfish with a damn cat's affection. I really do need to get out more.

"It's fine. I'm sorry I sounded so rude and ungrateful. He's used to me not working so I guess I've been letting the side down." I laugh, trying to lighten the mood.

"So, pizza?" he asks again.

I nod and follow him up the path and into his house.

It's spacious; he has minimal furniture in his living room, and what little he has is all pointed at a flat screen TV in the center. His house smells of him, fresh, like newly laundered washing. There are no photos of family, but there is an array of images of scenery from around town.

"These are great." I gesture to a cluster of images displaying the cornfields blowing in the wind, the pollen and seeds caught in the air in each frame.

He approaches me, handing me a glass of wine. "Red okay?"

I smile timidly up at him and take the glass with a thank you. "Are you a photographer?"

He's staring at me, studying every feature on my rosy-cheeked face. "I am, yes. Your skin would be so beautiful on camera."

My eyes widen and I choke a little on the gulp of red wine I guzzled while I wait for the okay to dive into the cheesy pizza topped with pepperoni and ham he has put on the table in front of the couch.

The silence that descends isn't uncomfortable. I'm trying to figure him out in the same way he must be doing to me, but he's quite the mystery. How is he single? He's gorgeous, considerate, clearly loves animals, and rescues damsels in distress by barging in with a gun when he hears screaming. He gardens and is a handyman around the house. Sigh.

"Why are you not married?" Oh my God, I've done a Tricia. No freaking filter; it's the red wine.

He sinks down on the couch and swigs at the glass. I'm assuming it's bourbon inside. The honey colored liquid disappears and is quickly refilled.

"I've never found the right woman, though I wasn't really looking either, which is usually when it happens, or so I'm told." He grabs a slice of pizza, the stringy cheese stretching from the rest before breaking away. He moans when it goes into his mouth and gestures with his foot for me to help myself. "What about you?"

"Me?"

He chuckles at my greed for food; my brain stopped registering anything other than pizza as soon as he picked up his slice. I shovel a mouthful in and groan when the flavors disperse over my tongue. "So good."

"Why aren't you married?" he asks, taking another bite of his slice.

"Because I'm so desirable to a husband? Have you seen the way I eat? The skittish behavior, and the way I'm clingy over my cat?"

We both chuckle and I'm relaxed and comfortable in his presence. It's such a huge step for me. I want to celebrate it and scream it from the rooftop.

After a couple more slices and another glass of red wine, my body tells me it's time for bed. Thanking Devon for the lovely evening, I make my way home.

Twenty-Six

Nina

THE WEEK PASSES WITH BUTTERFLIES present in my stomach. Every night, Devon or I bring dinner for the other, and Devon keeps making reference to this night being a date, despite the nerves coiling deep in my stomach. I know he won't expect anything from the end of the night, and it's comforting knowing I don't have that pressure. He doesn't know what happened to me but he knows something is different with me and he doesn't press for answers, he just accepts that I need to build trust, friendship, and that's really all I'm able to offer.

I catch Devon's grin when he senses my excitement. He pulls into an empty space in the designated field for parking. "Ready?"

I nod eagerly, returning his grin before I clamber out of his car. The air is already heady with smells of burgers and hotdogs, candy and popcorn. There's a variety of people milling around, loud noises and shouts echoing around us. The whole town is decked with bunting, and a mass of stalls are selling handmade goods, cakes and various second hand knickknacks.

My eyes won't keep still as we meander along the main street that's been cordoned off for the festival, my greedy gaze trying to mop up everything as we walk slowly.

I look up at the sky to a fairground ride when the sound of screams makes me jump. The carriages swing in the breeze and different colored legs dangle from each rocking chair.

"You like the Ferris wheel?" Devon asks as I gawp up at it.

"I used to as a child," I reply, stiffening slightly when he grabs my hand and pulls me to the short queue waiting to get on.

"So early?" I laugh at his eagerness.

He smiles, his crystal bright eyes flicking away. "I've never been on one. I'm not ashamed to admit I'm excited."

My mouth falls open with shock. "Seriously?"

He nods, openly admitting his shame as his cheeks redden slightly. "I was never allowed to go with Noah."

"Noah?"

I don't miss how he tenses but his hand remains in mine. "My brother."

I'm surprised by his revelation but when I go to question him again, the ride supervisor gestures us into a waiting car. Devon hesitates but I smile in encouragement and pull him gently. "Come on." I laugh. "It's my turn to protect you now."

He scowls playfully as we both settle into the hard seats. "Oh come on," he mocks, with a glint in his eye. "And what are you gonna do when the Big Bad Wolf comes, Little Red Riding Hood?"

I feign indignation and pull his belt across his lap, securing him in. I hate the sudden weightiness between us. If this were a movie there'd be some superimposed sparks igniting furiously around us, but it isn't and I'm not some kickass heroine, either. "I'll have you know, my singing is as agonizing as pulling teeth."

He snorts, then grabs for me when the ride starts and our car jolts. "So you're just gonna sing and the baddie will run away?"

I nod firmly. "See." I scrunch up my nose and take a sly peek at him. "I have it all worked out. Fear nothing when you're with me. I'm just going to say, you will never see Batman and me in the same place at the same time."

He stares at me then starts to laugh loudly. "Why, Nina, are you trying to tell me you have a secret?"

I can't help but swallow at the sudden twist in my gut. Staring down to the ground when we reach the height, I mumble, "If only you knew."

He looks at me curiously, but when a gust of wind catches our carriage and it rolls heavily, Devon squeals like a girl. I can't help but laugh at him, the horror on his face is comical. Then a thought occurs to me and I narrow my eyes at him, "Please don't tell me you're afraid of heights?" He grimaces, confirming my suspicions, and I stare at him. "Then why the hell did you come on the Ferris wheel?"

He shrugs, giving me a small smile. "Because I know you wanted to."

The air shifts around me and I can't seem to drag my eyes away from him. He is willing to scare the life out of himself just so he can see a smile on my face. A lump forms in my throat and for a long moment I can't seem to take a breath. His cheeks are red with embarrassment but eventually he turns to look back at me.

"Why?" My voice is a whisper, and with the noise of the wind in our ears, I'm not entirely sure he's heard me, but when he slowly reaches out with his hand, I can't move. His soft touch on my face disables me, my heart the only thing that's moving.

"Because you have the most beautiful smile."

This time it's my cheeks that heat, his gentle words turning the excitement from the ride into a different kind of excitement. He's staring at me, his eyes locked on mine, his soft lips parted to allow for his frantic breaths. My mouth dries when his fingers move from my cheek and into my hair.

He leans towards me and I know he's going to kiss me but I don't know if I want him to. My heart is racing, my belly throbbing, but the closer he gets, the more my body trembles, each hair that covers every inch of my skin standing to attention.

The car jolts again as we start to move back towards the ground and I quickly pull back. He blinks at me, a small frown creasing his forehead, but he smiles softly.

Guilt pours through me when I see the disappointment in his eyes, so I take his hand and slip my fingers through his. "I'm sorry, I'm a bit . . . apprehensive about this kind of thing."

He frowns harder but shakes his head. "Don't be silly. I would never push you into anything, Nina."

I smile. "Thank you."

He nods. "I know you're really shy, and you've been through some shit, but please tell me if I'm way off the mark."

The car comes to a stop at the bottom and we both climb off. Devon politely thanks the operator as he keeps my hand tight in his and leads me away from the ride. "Where would you like to go next?" he asks, not waiting for me to answer his last question.

I grin at his fervor. He's like a child at Christmas and I wonder if he's ever been to a fairground before. Then it gets me thinking about what his childhood was like, but as I open my mouth to ask him, he pulls me over to a stall selling the most enormous cupcakes. Each is different, in a vast array of colors and flavors, decorated in a different way to any other, and all covered with a variety of toppings.

Devon narrows his eyes at me. "Pick one but don't tell me which one."

I smile and look towards the dozens of cakes, my eyes hungrily devouring each one as I scan for one that stands out. "Hmm," I muse.

The seller behind the stall smiles at us both, her attention on us as I gaze across the bright colors. Another couple is stood to one side of us, and an elderly lady is watching our game with deep interest as another couple sidles up.

"Oh, come on, slow coach," Devon urges with a playful nudge.

"Hey, don't rush me. This is a matter of great importance. It has to be the right one."

I grin when I spot 'the one' and turn to Devon. "Okay, clever boy. Go for it!"

He nods seriously as if this is a mission of government standards then turns his gaze to the cakes and takes a deep breath. His bright eyes roam over each one, once or twice flicking back to a particular one that jumps out at him but then he stops and grins. "Got it!"

"Ahh, hang on," the seller cuts in, holding her hand up before she hands us both a small scrap of paper and a pen. "Write it down, then there's no cheating."

Devon laughs loudly. "How rude, Ma'am. I am a man of integrity." I quirk an eyebrow at him, silently reminding him of the stolen plants. "Okay." He chuckles as he grabs his own piece of paper and pen then gestures for me to turn around. On doing so, I shiver when he places the paper on my back and writes something down. Then he turns around and I place my own paper on his back and write down my answer.

The seller grins when we hand them over, her eyes looking at our answers. She chuckles, her lips pursing as she looks up at Devon. "For that, you can have it for free." She leans over and picks up the cake I chose then gives it to Devon, who grins and fist pumps the air.

"I knew it!"

I laugh when he hands me the cupcake with the white cat on it. "Clever boy!" I praise with laughter as our audience applauds Devon. Without thinking, I reach up and kiss him.

He's shocked, his faint gasp heating my lips, but within seconds he melts into me, his arms sliding around my back so he can pull me closer. His mouth is soft and warm, his breath coming in short sharp stutters as a small moan grumbles in his chest. His lips press harder, our needs reaching new levels when his hands frame my face. His kiss is strong and passionate but full of feeling, his sudden control making me gasp and pull back.

He stares at me for a moment then a huge smile breaks free and he licks his lips as if he can still taste me. "I'm hungry," he says, his eyes twinkling.

The audience applauds our kiss and the heat that flames my cheeks could poach an egg. Devon laughs and grabs my hand. "Come on, I need feeding!" He waves to the cake seller and thanks her before pulling me over to a hotdog stand.

It's dark when Devon pulls up in his driveway. Steve is sitting on the small wall between our houses.

"Oh, that reminds me," Devon says. "Steve has still been visiting me while you've been at work. I think we need to sort out a custody agreement. You can have him Mondays, Wednesdays, Fridays and every other weekend, and I'll take the rest." He winks.

I smile and shake my head, rolling my eyes at Steve's

cheekiness. "Don't tell me, my poor frail boy wanted feeding again?"

Devon laughs and nods. "Yup."

Climbing out of the car, I call Steve and he comes sauntering over, wrapping his furry body around me. "Thank you for today, it's been wonderful."

Devon nods but his face is serious as he reaches out and takes my hand, softly linking his fingers through mine. "You want to come in?"

My mouth dries and I blow out a breath. "I don't . . . really think that's wise."

He nods then grins mischievously. "Why? Am I in danger? Do you lure men to the fairground and then entice them back with cotton candy to rape them?"

His eyes widen in shock when he sees the blood drain from my face and I shake my head wildly.

"Shit, Nina, I'm sorry. I didn't mean for that to . . . crap! What I meant was . . . I was just joking." He looks to the floor and sighs, his mortification bright on his face. "Me and my stupid mouth. I'm sorry."

I blink at his overdramatic apology. My heart beats furiously as I stare at him.

"You know." There's only one reason he would react like that, and that's if he knows how far he shoved his foot in his mouth.

He sighs and closes his eyes before opening them and looking at me. "I don't know anything, but, well I can kind of tell that you've been hurt . . . bad. I made assumptions, and by the reaction I just got, I presume I'm right."

I don't know how to react. I'm furious that he's been making assumptions about me, but then, I'm also faintly pleased I've been in his thoughts. I'm angry that I'm obviously so open and I'm ashamed by my inability to be honest with people. I'm scared of what Devon will think yet I'm hopeful that it won't change anything in our new friendship. I like him, he makes me laugh, and I've smiled a lot more often since he'd moved in.

"It was a long time ago," I manage to choke out.

His eyes darken and I'm unsure if it's with rage or sadness. "I'm not going to say it's time to move on, Nina, because frankly, it's only you that knows when the time is right. But I will say that I'm here. Just here. I have no motives, no plan B, or any plans come to that. I will be here tomorrow," he whispers, "And I'll be here the day after that and every day, just to be in your presence."

"Why?" I whisper, my lids dropping as I look up at him.

He leans in and tenderly kisses my cheek, before he runs his fingertip across my jaw. "Because you're Batman, and that's freaking cool." He gives me a wicked wink and grins then walks away to the sound of my giggle.

I stand and watch him disappear into his house. It's only when a drop of rain lands on my nose and Steve meows loudly that I turn and walk into my own.

Twenty-Seven

Devon

I LOVE THE SMELL OF grass the morning after it's rained all night. The sun bright in the sky makes the droplets look like crystals. It's as if nature is starting again, cleansing the world of its dirt.

Grabbing my camera, I go into the garden where Nina is sitting with the coffee she fetched from the local diner earlier, along with breakfast bagels. My heart thunders against my ribcage when I hold the lens to my eye and look through to see her smiling at me. Her body is so close. The smile isn't one from afar directed at someone else, or one I've been paid to document. This one is all mine, and it's breath-taking. She's so unique. Perfect.

"You're your own kind of beautiful. Nothing comes close to you."

Her full plump lips drop open and a tear bubbles in her eye. She doesn't let it drop, she giggles and swipes it away, and it's then that I wish I'd picked up the camcorder so I captured the sound as well as the image of her laughing, so carefree. She reaches forward and grabs the end of the extended scope with both hands then kisses the lens. "You're the beautiful one. I wish the world was full of more gentle souls like you."

I almost choke on my own saliva with her words. She's blind to the dark shadow always following me, its relentlessness, making my soul far from beautiful. To her, I'm Devon; nice, normal, worthy of her trust, and hopefully, her heart. My sweet Nina is fearful of the world around her but forgiving to it, she has let herself trust again, that works in my favor.

I take the seat next to her and she automatically slips her hand into mine and lets them hang between us. My chest constricts and I'm happy for the first time in a long, long time . . . *since Courtney.*

"You need to perk up your pansies." My eyes flutter at her statement, and for a second I think she's mocking me for feeling giddy about the handholding. "By your window." She gestures to the kitchen window, which looks over the backyard. The plants I planted there are all keeling over. "Maybe the sun isn't reaching them?" she offers, but that's not the case. They've been trodden on . . . *Noah. NOAH!*

"I need to go to work." She sighs.

I raise our joined hands and kiss hers, causing her to

suck in her bottom lip. I want to suck on it. I want to suck, bite and experience all she has to offer. "I'll drive you," I say, making her chuckle.

"Why? I have a car."

I tug her arm, causing her to stumble from her seat onto my lap. She gasps but her body soon relaxes into mine. "So I have an excuse to pick you up later for dinner."

Her head drops to my shoulder and I hear her inhale my scent. "You smell like danger and excitement all in one . . . how is that possible?"

"Danger is exciting, but the only one in danger here is me."

"Really? Why? Because I'm batman?" she quips, bringing her face from the crook of my neck to look into my eyes.

"No, because you disarm me, intoxicate and utterly beguile me. I'm in danger of losing my heart to you and you not wanting it." I can almost see the beat of her heart through her chest.

Her hand lays over mine so she can feel the intensity of its beat. "I do want it," she whispers. "And I pray that I don't hurt it." She leans down and takes my lips with her own. The taste of coffee and cream cheese has never tasted so good.

I miss work. It's depraved and sinful, but the craving to film and document is more real to me than food and water. It's more a necessity than air but not more powerful than the need to have Nina, so I drink whiskey and take pictures of scenery. I've walked to the lake a mile from my house to get some shots of the water. I plan to make a collage for Nina's room, which is unembellished and rather depressing.

My lips tingle with thoughts of her, and I smile to myself. I'm crazy in love with that woman and she's falling for me too. I've never been more ready to catch someone.

The grass is long, left wild to grow and border the lake which sits still like a pane of glass, the sun's reflection giving the surface a sparkle that reminds me of Nina's eyes. The heat of the afternoon sun burns through my clothing and causes everything in the distance to look slightly disjointed, as if it's a reflection in the lake and a wave is ever so gently rippling across.

I shoot some birds soaring high in the cloudless sky, and some rabbits playing on the flatter part of greenery. It's like a fairy-tale, this place. I've fallen into a scene from Snow White. My nerve endings tingle, and nervous, excited energy surges in my gut. *And there is Snow White.*

A dark-haired girl dances across the river. She's thick in the thighs and tiny on top. Her clothes leave her in abandon. She giggles and screams when her feet hit the water.

Picking up my camera, the touch of it so right in my damp palm, I zoom in. The gradual draw excites me; it's almost as if I'm pulling her to me on some invisible rope. The magic the lens grants makes my mouth water. She's wearing white cotton panties but her small pert breasts are on display, her nipples hard and dark. She has a sprinkle of moles down her stomach, disappearing into her briefs. She's looking behind her, over her shoulder, and screeching for someone to join her. A broad guy fills the frame and I pull away to make sure there's not a crowd of them and that nobody can spot me, but it's just those two and I'm isolated in my viewing.

I click the camera, documenting every part of her. The guy throws his t-shirt to the floor and kicks off his pants and his underwear; he's in shape and around twenty if I was to guess. His broad shoulders indicate he plays sports or lifts weights. His dick hangs between his thighs and slaps side to side like a dead fish as he wades into the lake and kicks up water to soak Snow White, eliciting a scream and a cuss from her thin-lipped mouth. Her panties dampen and show the unkempt hair beneath. Reaching out, he grabs her and plunges them both beneath the surface, causing a ripple to spread like a tidal wave.

When he resurfaces, she's wrapped around him and they're kissing. Walking back to the shoreline with her tightly draped around him, he drops to his knees and she pushes from him, lying on her back. I capture them so closely that the goose bumps decorating their skin is caught in the image. He leans over to his jeans, pulls out a condom, and slips it on. Not bothering to remove her wet panties he pulls them aside and rams straight into her.

Click.

Her face contorts in discomfort.

Click.

His body thrusts against her, his ass cheeks tensing and squeezing together.

Click.

Her face relaxes and she guides his hips, lifting her own legs higher.

Click.

He rubs at her small nipples like they're a magic lamp and a genie is going to pop out. I almost feel sorry for Snow White.

Click.

And he shudders and collapses over her.

I capture her eye roll on film and let my mind wander into the plan Noah could cook up for her. I hate that I miss him.

A chill rouses me from sleep. My eyes open and I'm a little discombobulated. *What the? Crap!* I fell asleep at the lake. I look at my watch and cuss. I have ten minutes before I have to pick Nina up and I haven't made reservations anywhere.

Grabbing my stuff, I jog back to the house, regretting bringing two heavy as shit cameras with me as they hit me in the back the entire run home. I'm sweating and need to quickly make a change of clothes. I push open the front door, run up to my room and freeze.

No . . . No . . . NO.

A pool of blood stains my duvet, and in the middle of it, Steve lays with his throat slit. My guts somersault inside me and instinctively my hand slaps over my mouth as I stare wide-eyed at the bloody mess. My head feels fuzzy.

I'm frozen solid and can't pull my mind into focus. Nina will think I did this and she'll run again. Damn it, she loves that cat. He's harmless, and my friend, and that's why he killed him. I'm not allowed anyone but him.

I need to dispose of Steve and hope Nina thinks he moved on to another household.

Twenty-Eight

Nina

I'M HUMMING. ME! AND NOT just the sound either. My whole body feels light, featherweight, and I'm lifting from the ground and floating on cloud nine. The guys have noticed my chipper mood and quiz me, but I give nothing away. I'm keeping hold of the emotions I'm feeling. I'm keeping Devon in a box only for my knowledge. Tricia has been questioning me about him non-stop in our nightly calls but I play it off. I don't want her throwing smut on what's happening between us. I love that girl but she thinks with her lady dick. My thoughts cause a chuckle to bubble out of me and Gerry quirks a brow; I interrupted him eating a pink frosted doughnut. Mmm, that looks good, actually.

I check the time and excitement races through my veins. Only thirty minutes left and Devon will be taking me to dinner . . . *out in public*. I push down my reservations and agree with myself that I'm going to go with the moment instead of living in fear of what could happen.

"No, Mrs. Perry, it's not a crime if you allowed him to have a key." I try and reason with the old lady who makes my day exhausting at least twice a week.

"He won't give it back."

"Okay, Ma'am, this is what I'm going to do. I'm going to call for someone to come and change the locks, and this time don't give your son a key."

"Oh, that would be perfect, Tina, because . . ." It annoys me when she purposely gets my name wrong out of spite, and no doubt she will give that boy a key and ring me to whine about it.

"I have another call, Mrs. Perry. Have a good evening." I end the call to the sound of Gerry's chuckle. I grab a doughnut and launch it at him, which he catches in mock horror.

"Never risk a doughnut dropping on the floor, Nina," he scolds, seriously.

"You're such a cop." I laugh, shaking my head at his red face.

Luke's heavy boots clunk across the old wooden floors as he enters with a prisoner in tow, the first one I've ever seen arrested. "Gerry, book Mr. Gates in for the night."

"I wwanna goo hoeeem," the drunk man slurs, stumbling forward and crashing his fists down on the desk.

"Where'd you find him this time?" Gerry asks.

"In the Miller's stables, trying to molest their prize horse."

Gerry and I both groan out a, "What the hell?"

The scent trail left from the animal perv makes my nose twitch. Luke leans over my desk, tapping his finger against the clock. He smells of leather and man sweat. It's not pungent, but gentle and unique to him. I sigh at the time. Thirty minutes late. I debate waiting but decide against it. I don't want to have to walk home in the dark if he doesn't show.

"I'm leaving now," I tell him.

He grabs my purse and sweater from the hook on the wall behind me. "I'll take you home. I wanted to speak to you anyway." I'm relieved to have a ride and offer him a small smile in thanks.

The seats are hot from the sun. It's uncomfortable and I feel a little guilty having him drive me home. He works way too many hours.

"What is it you want to ask me?" I ask, trying to get him to stop looking at me with worry. I'm grateful he's compassionate towards me for what happened but he has enough people to worry about. Adding my load to his list isn't fair.

"I'm taking tomorrow off."

"Oh?"

"I'm going to your old address."

My body stiffens. "What? Why?"

"I want to take a look around Mr. Ilavich's house. I can't find it listed anywhere for sale, only the handmade sign out front." My head buzzes as I try to focus on him. "Nina, in your file it says you checked out of the hospital the next day. Did you go home? Was he still living there?"

I shake my head, my mouth going dry. "I didn't check out. My injuries were too severe, but the police told the hospital to have me down as discharged if anyone called or came in. They staked out my house for two weeks, hoping he'd return there."

"So when did you go back?"

"I didn't. I had Tricia pack up the house when the police gave up and I moved here straight from hospital."

"So you never saw him again?"

I shake my head and squeeze my hands together in my lap until my knuckles turn white. His warm hand covers them. "I'm sorry if I'm bringing up old scars, Nina. I'm the sheriff, and sometimes it's hard to switch that off."

The car barely stops and I jump out, shouting, "It's fine, Luke. Thanks for the ride home," as I shut the door behind me.

Luke pulls away and I wait for his headlights to fade out of sight before taking a few deep breaths to give myself courage to go over to Devon's and ask why he didn't come for me. My feet stomp up his front steps, my small fist balling and banging against the wood of the door, but I get no answer.

I stomp back the way I came, and before I make it to my side entrance, a flash in my peripheral view has me turning to Devon's backyard. I open the gate and halt at the scene in front of me. Devon is shirtless, and covered in mud. Sweat glistens all over him and he looks kind of manic, patting down soil where once his pansies were.

"Devon?" I call, but it's like he's deaf. His head eventually tilts up but it's like he sees straight through me. I step back and call his name again.

Twenty-Nine

Devon

It's like looking through glazed glass. My vision is blurry and the sound penetrating my ears is distorted and sounds far away. I managed to collect Steve up in the duvet and sheet but I'll need a new mattress. I ripped the flower bed up under the window where Noah had trodden down the flowers.

"Devon?"

Nina. Shit, Nina!

Dropping the shovel, I brush the dirt from my chest. "Oh my God, Nina?"

"Devon, are you okay? You look a little out of it?"

I'm sad and annoyed and . . . *What the hell? I'm hallucinating.*

"Hey there, big guy. Are you hungry?"

It's Steve. She picks him up. I look down at the flower bed and back to her arms.

"Devon? Are you okay? You didn't pick me up."

I shake my head and walk over to her and Steve, rubbing my palm down his fur, and I'm rewarded with a loud purr. "I'm so sorry. I didn't realize the time."

"You have blood on your jeans."

I look down to the patch of blood, and back up into her worried eyes. "I reopened my cut with a pair of scissors as I opened the compost bag." I reassure her. "Let me take a quick shower and I'll take you for some dinner." I smile and lean in to drop a kiss against her lips. Her breathy sigh ignites the fire in me.

"Just shower and then come over. I've had a busy day. What do you say to me cooking my famous omelet?" She grins and everything feels right again.

"I'd say that sounds perfect."

She returns my smile and I jolt when her thumb swipes across my top lip. She chuckles, wiping the piece of dirt she collected between her thumb and finger and then turns away, Steve plodding happily behind her. I can't help but blow out a relieved breath at the sight of him.

"Scruff," she shouts to me. "Hurry up. The eggs are only good until the end of next week!"

Holding my hands up when she winks over her shoulder at me, I blow her a kiss and turn back to my house. "I'm going, I'm going!"

She gives me a mile wide smile when I compliment her

omelet. "My God, you weren't joking. Woman, this is seriously good."

"Of course it is. I made it!" She winks and places her cutlery to one side, the half of her leftover omelet taunting me. Catching my gaze she tuts and lifts her plate, sliding her food onto mine.

"So, what have you been up to today?" she asks as she places her plate into the basin and turns the faucet on full blast. She squeals and jumps back when the jet of water hits her fork and sprays across the kitchen and down the front of her.

She gawps, the water continuing to gush out and pour onto the floor. I can't help but laugh at her shock as I reach over her and shut off the faucet. She blinks up at me, her long eyelashes dripping, and her red cheeks wet and flushed. "Are you always this . . . ?"

She narrows her eyes on me but I can see the amusement glistening back at me. "Don't you dare say it!" she warns, trying to keep her soft lips straight and her face stern.

" . . . Graceful?" I laugh.

Her mouth falls open in shock but for the longest moment I can't seem to breathe. Her white dress is wet and clings to her stunning body. Her dark nipples poke through, teasing my cock so much that my pants don't seem to be able to confine its sudden swell. My chest begins to ache with longing, and automatically, my tongue teases my bottom lip.

Dropping her face to see what has caught my attention, Nina slowly looks back up at me. Something in her eyes makes me step forwards. Her breathing is erratic and heavy, her chest heaving with every deep pull.

"I better go," I whisper, my voice coming out quiet and restrained against the constriction of lust in my throat. But when I turn to leave, her hand whips out and her fingers curl around my wrist. The air between us is stifling, the lack of oxygen making it difficult to breathe.

"I don't want you to go," she whispers.

My skin prickles with goose bumps, however I manage to reach out and softly hold the side of her face. "Nina, I'm perfectly fine to wait. For however long you need it to be."

"I know," she says quietly. "But I don't think I am. I want to feel again, Devon. I want to feel good again."

Her words don't register at first but when they do I blink at her. "Are you saying you want to . . . ?"

"I want you to make love to me," she finishes for me. She smiles and nods, "I'm ready. And I want to feel you."

If it wasn't for the honesty in her eyes I would pull back, but her gaze is soft and her smile is relaxed. My heart pounds frantically in my chest, excitement pouring through me as I lean down and kiss her. Her hands immediately come around me, her fingers digging into the muscles on my back as she holds onto me like her life depends on it.

The way she kisses me back tells me everything. I can feel her conviction, her need, as potently as if it's my own. Her fingers are wrestling with my shirt buttons as she deepens our kiss, her tongue teasing my own as her arousal grows fiercer. "Please," she whispers when she slides the material off my shoulders and her fingers softly roam down the front of my bare chest. "Please, Devon."

Thirty

Nina

"I want this to be all you, Nina," he whispers, as his fingers softly trace along the edge of my jaw. "Take your clothes off for me." His tone is laced in lust, the control cracking on delivery.

I want this so much, my body begging me for its moment. It needs the release, the tenderness I know Devon can give me. I'm falling in love with him. I'm not stupid enough to tell him that, but for the first time in over a year, I completely trust a man. I see the way he looks at me, the way his eyes soften every time they fall on me. I know how he feels for me, and because of that, he has given me something back that has been taken for so long. I want to step over into the next part of my life. I want to finally live and feel alive.

I slip the dress straps from my shoulders and let it pool to the floor in a puddle of fabric. My nipples are hard and tingling with anticipation. I'm nervous about him seeing me laid bare, all my scars angry and ugly, showing him how broken I am, and I wrap my arms around my torso to hide me . . . *to comfort me.*

"You're so beautiful." The awe in his voice makes my heart beat a little quicker and my anxiousness dissolves a tiny bit.

He strips from his own pants and shorts, and I have to count in my head to stop myself from blurting out he's too big and I'm scared.

He takes a few steps towards me, his hand reaching out and gliding over my skin so softly it's like silk being draped over me. Pulling my arms away from my body, he inhales a breath, the tips of his fingers tracing the scars left permanently fused in my skin. "You're like a piece of art, Nina. Colorful and vibrant. Each stroke of you tells a story." His chest beats out of rhythm, his heavy pants in symmetry to my own. "I want to photograph you and keep you forever."

I blush furiously at his idolization as he drops to his knees and directs my body to turn. My feet hesitantly obey, giving him the view of my back. Kisses akin to a feather being pulled over my flesh rain over my lower back, and his tongue swipes out to trace each mark, claiming them and changing what they mean. He finds me beautiful, despite the raised, broken flesh I always see as damage.

His mouth hovers over my backside, and when his

tongue licks up the crease I jump in surprise. He chuckles, and it's deep, reaching the ache in my core. "I want to taste every inch of you, claim your body, mind and soul as my own. I want to fuse your scent, touch, and flavor, your sound when you moan, into every sense I own. I want to devour you until all you know is how fucking perfect and special you are, how beautiful and worthy you are of affection, love and kindness. How indescribable your essence is."

My body shakes from the emotions clogging up my heart and throat. His words are becoming too much to cope with, along with how vulnerable my body feels.

"Tell me what you want Nina. This is all you."

"I want to feel beautiful again, I want you to see a desirable woman and not a victim who's scared of what you'll see when you look at me."

His head shakes. "All I see is beauty and strength, and you're sexy as hell in a way no one compares to. You're everything any man could ever want when he sees the naked form of a woman."

"I need you to take control, Devon. Tell me what you want me to do."

"I want you to lie on the table. I want you to drop your thighs, and let me look at all of your beauty. Let me show you how to love you again, how to appreciate all that perfect you have going on, Nina, because to me, you're so perfect. Can you do that?"

I nod and bite my lip, doing as he asks although every inch of me is trembling. His words give me the strength I need to get past this barrier. Keeping myself locked away and from feeling, loving, living isn't a life. I bite my inner cheek so hard from my nerves that it tastes like I'm sucking on a battery when the blood fills my mouth and trickles down my throat.

"You're breath taking. I want to love every part of you. Can I taste you?"

I only manage a small squeak in answer because his words are overwhelming me with emotion. He makes me feel like a rare diamond, beautiful, with my own sparkle. He leans forward, his hair tickling my inner thighs as he takes a deep inhale and I try to close my legs on instinct.

"You can deny me if you're not ready, but if it's just nerves and you want this, then let me show you how to feel good again," he pleads. It's like he knows me better than myself.

"I want this" I breathe.

"Lean up onto your elbows for me." I swallow hard and rise up on my elbows, looking down at him through heavy lids. He is so handsome, his sculptured cheekbones and his strong jaw making me need him to touch me even more. "Use one hand to support yourself and the other to grip my hair. Direct me between your sweet thighs and show me what feels good. Use me to get off, Nina."

I'm torn between crying and screaming out in bliss. I grasp a handful of his soft locks and pull him closer to me so his lips press against the pink flesh glistening with the arousal he has pulled from me. He opens his mouth and very slowly licks over me. My head drops back as ecstasy ripples through me and my hips push forwards for more pressure. I can't help but tug him closer, and he laps at my opening, tasting all I have to offer as his tongue pushes inside me, swirling, prodding, and completely devouring me. I maneuver him up towards my throbbing clit and he takes the hint, twirling his tongue over the sensitive bud.

"Feel me against your perfect pink clit, Nina. Grind on me as hard as you need. Feel it building. It's all you, baby." His words are like an explosion of desire too hot to contain. I moan out, rotating my hips and riding his face while pushing him so hard against me it's almost painful.

He grips me under the ass and lifts me further against him, worshipping me with his mouth. My stomach tightens, flooding with warmth when my inner walls throb and contract and I cry out my orgasm. My legs are weak and my whole body feels like molten lava melting into the table. He quickly swipes me up into his arms and carries me through to the lounge and over to the couch. He lies on his back with me laid out on top of him. "I want you to feel me fill you up, Nina. Ride me to make yourself come again. Use me. Let me feel you over me. I want you to take me. I'm yours, all of me."

Guiding my body down over his hard cock, I inhale sharply at the sensation. It's been so long, and the sensations of having a man inside me again are a little overwhelming. "Take your time, Nina," Devon says as he stares up at me. The look of amazement, pleasure and need in his eyes causes me to shudder over him. Emotions encompass me and my body molds with his, our sweat and skin merging us as one entity. His hold on me is fierce and protective as he glides my hips up and down his length. Pleasure roars inside me and it takes me by surprise. I never imagined being this way with anyone after the rape. I didn't think I could ever feel the overwhelming pleasure ricocheting through every nerve ending, coiling in my core and sparking quivers through my veins. Every upward thrust of his pelvis touches deeper inside me and I'm floating away on a consciousness of ecstasy.

Thirty-One

Devon

I'M INSIDE HER, FEELING THE warmth of her inner walls clenching around my cock and soaking me in the release I caused her to have. Her scars scatter over her like a jigsaw puzzle dismantled and then put back together. She's beautiful in her marred skin. No matter what he did to her, he can't take that from her. Her soul is bright and glorious, causing her skin to almost glow from its intensity. Every strand of her hair falls like silk over her pale, creamy flesh. Her bright eyes dance with anticipation and nervous energy. Her dark rose budded nipples peak to perfection and her low breathy tone makes my dick twitch and rise to greet the plea in her voice.

Giving over control gave her a sense of power that Noah had once stripped her of; she rode my tongue with abandon and flooded my mouth, her amazing essence bursting on my tongue and lighting a fire so fierce I almost lost it before getting inside her.

Her scent as her body mists with a sheen of sweat entices me further. I can't get deep enough inside the heat of her body; nothing will ever be enough when it comes to her. It's a profound emotion after watching, waiting and yearning for her for so long, and now to have her in my arms, under my tongue and over my cock brings such an intense climax that my eyes close and my body tenses as I explode, filling her up as I roar out her name.

She cries out above me, my climax forcing another orgasm to drive pleasure through her. I want to give her more and more, give her nothing but bliss and heaven.

"Devon!" she shouts as her back arches and her tits thrust upwards. I can't help but reach up and pinch her nipples, prolonging her orgasm as it floods over my balls and thighs. Her face is so stunning right at this moment that it causes my chest to stutter, my heart unable to cope with the rush of hormones that my body is frantically forcing through me.

"I'm here, Nina," I cry with her, her pleasure making my own orgasm more intense. "I'm here."

She gasps and drops forwards, her cheek settling on my chest as she fights for breath and composure. My arms instinctively surround her, her warmth and my heat merging together and refusing our drenched bodies any relief.

"Oh wow," she whispers, and her body shudders with emotion at the same time, her hand tucking under her chin and on my chest. "Thank you." A tear slips onto her cheek and the intensity in her eyes holds so much power over me that my own eyes mist over.

I tilt her chin back with my finger and study her face.

"Are you okay?"

She blinks at me and for a moment I think she's going to sob but she takes a deep breath and nods. "Okay? I'd say I'm utterly freaking fantastic."

I sigh and kiss her nose, sliding my hand into hers. "Yes, you are. Although I would have said utterly *fucking* fantastic. My God, I've never . . ." I grimace, blushing at my own soppiness.

She grins. "Yeah, me too." Snuggling into me, she yawns. "I'm exhausted."

I nod, agreeing with her as her yawn triggers my own. Steve jumps onto the couch and spins round and round on Nina's back. I can't help but chuckle at him when he finally settles down.

A shiver races through me when my thoughts go to the cat who is buried under the pansies. It doesn't make sense. The only reasoning is that Noah got the wrong cat. It had been the same grey and build as Steve, probably a litter of his knowing him, but luckily, it wasn't Nina's beloved feline.

Wondering why Nina isn't shooing him off or complaining, I look down. She's asleep. With me still inside her. She looks so peaceful and beautiful that I don't move her.

So there we sleep. Steve on top of Nina, and Nina on top of me. My heart clenches when a word shimmers in my head. A word I had given up on a long time ago.

Family.

I wake to the smell of frying bacon and pancakes. My grumbling stomach is apparently more awake than I am when I roll over and land on the floor with a thud. "Shit!" I grumble, rubbing at my forehead.

"You're bleeding!" Nina gasps from where she's appeared by the door. I don't hear what she says as my eyes roam down every perfect inch of her. She's wearing my white cotton dress shirt—and nothing else. The outline of her perfect breasts press against the sheer material, her dark rich nipples making my mouth water for something other than breakfast.

She hurries over and kneels beside me, grabbing a handful of tissues from a small box on the table and pressing them to the gash on my brow. "And you say I'm a calamity." She giggles.

I growl at her, my hands gripping her waist. I flip her until she's completely laid out under me. "Less talk and more worship, woman!"

She gawps at me but when my lips move up her neck she whimpers and stirs beneath me. My cock is already hard and pressing into her stomach. "But I'm hungry," she breathes.

"Me too," I murmur as I reach her lips and devour her. She's as sweet as the pancakes I know she's making, her taste even better than any food that's available on this planet.

Nudging her legs open with my knee I'm inside her in seconds, both of us groaning appreciatively at the tight fill. She's already wet for me and I can feel her juices cover me. "Oh God," she mumbles, her breath in my ear making me shiver.

"He's busy right now, so you got me instead."

She giggles and swats at me but then releases a long moan when I grind my hips against her and push deeper. Her fingertips dig into my bare ass as she tries to pull me in more. Her eyes flutter closed and her lips part.

"You are so fucking beautiful," I groan as I start a relentless rhythm inside her, my hips bucking hard and urgently.

"Harder," she moans, begging me. "Harder, Devon."

She surprises me but I give her what she wants, thrusting deeper and faster until both of us are lost in a haze of erotic moans and words.

"Like this?" I growl as my balls tighten angrily and my spine tingles with heat. "You want it hard like this, Nina?" I'm driving her up the carpet with every fierce thrust, her back taking the grueling torture as her legs clamp around my waist and she lifts her hips with each of my pushes inside.

"Yes!" she cries out as her pussy clenches so hard I swear she's going to strangle my cock. I explode inside her, filling her up with the very parts of me that have always been reserved for her and only her.

Her nails rake down my back as her own release drives a painful pleasure through her, her teeth bared as her orgasm takes over and brings out her animalistic side. Fuck, she's even more beautiful right now, her raw beauty mesmerizing when I'm the one who is giving her the ecstasy that is tearing through her system.

"Oh, Jesus Christ," she puffs out.

"He's busy too. And to be honest, I don't think he'd be as good as me anyway."

She laughs, her twinkling eyes full of happiness. However, they widen when an alarm screeches, fracturing the quietness.

"Shit!" she gasps as she pushes me off her and jumps up. "The bacon!"

"Good job. I like it well done!" I shout after her with a laugh.

"Well done?" she scoffs from the kitchen. "It's freaking cremated."

I stand behind her and stare over her shoulder, the pan sizzling under the torrent of water where she's thrown it in the sink to put out the fire. She glances sideways at me and pouts. "I hope you're okay with just pancakes."

Laughing, I kiss her earlobe. "Get dressed. Breakfast's on me."

She nods slowly and sighs. "It might be best." Returning my kiss, she smiles then runs up the stairs.

I can't keep the grin off my face. I have never in a million years dreamed that life could be this good. She's more perfect than I imagined, her beauty mesmerizing and her sweet heart an honor to hold in my hand.

"Have you seen my hairbrush? I can't find it," she shouts down the stairs. I quirk a brow, pondering her question and wondering why in the hell I would have her brush, but then I hear her giggle when she has the very same thought. "No, I don't suppose you have."

Life is good. In fact, life is fucking perfect.

Thirty-Two

Devon

She's raking her fingers through her hair again, and grumbling. "Will you stop? It looks fine."

There are only two other customers in the coffee shop I've brought her to to make up for the breakfast I ruined earlier.

She sighs and pouts. "I hate having to go through it with a comb, it makes it all frizzy. And I have to go into work looking like this!"

"Nina." I chuckle around a forkful of bacon. "You sit behind a desk. Nobody in this dead town will even see you."

"That's not the point. It's my job and I should look presentable."

"But you do! You're beautiful. With or without a yeti attached to the top of your head."

She rolls her eyes and slaps me but the blush that

creeps over her cheeks is adorable. Smiling, she shrugs. "But you have to say that."

"Why?"

"Because you're my boyfriend."

My heart thuds so hard that I swear I'm having a coronary. My mouth dries and I struggle to form words. "Is that what I am?" My voice is quiet and I hate that I'm gazing at her with awe, but right now I don't care if the whole world is witnessing my weakness.

Her blush deepens. "Well, aren't you?" She seems timid and almost scared of my answer, but when I grin, she smiles that damn pretty smile that makes my heart rate quicken.

She nods firmly as if we've settled some major issue and takes a stab at her bacon. "I suppose we should get to know one another better."

I don't like where she's going and I pause with my fork halfway to my mouth. "Oh?"

"Mmm." She nods. "So, what's . . . your favorite color?"

I disguise the relieved breath that bursts from me and pretend to think. "Blue."

"Favorite movie?"

"Oh, that's easy. Reservoir Dogs."

She stares at me. "Too gory."

I laugh. "What's yours?"

"Don't judge!"

I shake my head and hold up my hands. "Scouts honor."

She narrows her eyes when I place the two fingers on my chest. "You weren't a scout!"

"I so was!" Her gaze is probing and I laugh. "Okay,

maybe not. But I wanted to be."

"Well, how come you didn't then?"

I shrug, sliding my fork through my pancake. "Just not something my parents approved of."

She looks at me for a moment then lowers her eyes to her plate. "Do you still see them?"

I shake my head, my body tensing slightly with the way our conversation has gone. "No, they're dead."

Her wide eyes lift to me and she reaches across the table to take my hand. The pity on her face is horrifying and I swallow back the need to tell her to stop looking at me like that. "I'm so sorry, Devon," she whispers. "Do you have any other family?"

Her questions are making the anger in my gut bubble. "I had a sister once, and now just a brother, but I don't see him."

"Why not?"

Because he wouldn't let me keep you. At one point I never thought I could live without him. I loved him and knew he was the only one who understood me because he lived what I had, and then he betrayed me and my head's been a mess ever since. I'm worried he will try and take you from me.

I don't voice any of this; instead I opt for changing the conversation.

"You know!" I quickly say. "I've been thinking about opening a gallery for my photographs."

Her sadness instantly disappears and her face brightens with my revelation. "Oh, what a wonderful idea. This place gets really busy in the summer season." She's clearly excited and I catch the bug. It had just been a lame quick-thinking statement to change the subject, but now I'm actually toying with the idea.

"You could set up a stand near the harbor, you know? Take family portraits for those on vacation who want to document their memories."

"That's a good idea. But what I would love to do is display images of you." I smile but rub at my temples when I feel a migraine coming on.

"What?" she stutters, trying to swallow the piece of pancake she's just shoved into her mouth.

"You're very photogenic, Nina. The contours of your face are every photographers dream come true. Not to mention your boyfriend's."

She stares at me but then shrugs. "Okay."

I'll admit, I'm slightly shocked by her agreement. I expected her to go to war with me over it but she looks nearly as eager as I am.

"Oh!" She gasps as she checks her watch. "I have to get to work."

I blink when my vision starts to spit blots in front of me.

"Are you okay?"

I open my eyes and smile at Nina, her concern making my heart swell. Throwing a twenty on the table, I take her elbow and lead her out of the coffee shop. "I'm fine. I think I have a migraine coming on."

"You should go back to bed. You're probably tired."

I chuckle and waggle my eyebrows at her as she slides into the passenger seat of my car. "Yeah, I didn't get too much sleep. This amazing woman with yeti hair kept me up all night." I shut the door quickly before she gives me one of her playful slaps.

"Really?" she continues when I climb in beside her. "You should have had my morning. God was busy so he sent one of his minions to give me a once over."

I stifle my laughter as I pull out of the lot. "He did, huh? And did you pass?"

She shrugs and sighs dramatically. "I have no idea. He had to send Jesus down for a second opinion but then he got held up as well so I had to settle with the underling once again."

"The underling, huh?"

"Mmm," she murmurs as if bored. "But it's God's work so I can't really refuse him, can I?"

"Oh no," I shake my head seriously. "You should never interfere with what God wants. In fact, I work for him and he told me this morning that I have a new mission to complete tonight."

Excitement lights her eyes. She squirms in her seat as her mind relays all sorts of 'missions'. "Oh, wow. You are so honored. What is this important mission?"

"Well, it involves you, so I'm sure I'll be okay to share."

"Oh, you can share. You can definitely share it with me."

Pulling up outside the Sheriff's office, I lean across the car and trickle the tip of my nose over the shell of her ear. She's liquid beneath me, her imagination driving her crazy. "Well, I need your help with this important matter." She nods, her chest heaving when I gently bite down on her earlobe. "We have to do something together."

"Oh, Christ," she murmurs when I dip my tongue out and trail it in a circle behind her ear.

"Yes, he asked me too, so that's how important it is. You see, Nina." She nods again. "He wants me to make you happy."

"Oh, that's good," she mumbles. "I agree with him."

I can't help but chuckle. "Mmm, he wants me to . . ."

"To?" she whimpers when I run my tongue down the front of her throat. "To?"

"He wants me to . . ." I drag my mouth back up and hover over her lips, " . . . to find your hairbrush." Before she can hit me, I slam my mouth on hers and kiss her. She slaps at me but it's weak as she kisses me back, her little whimpers making my dick hard and my headache dive towards the impending migraine.

Feeling me wince beneath her, she pulls back and cups my face. "Go home, take some meds, and sleep."

"Sounds good."

"Are you okay getting home? I can drive you first if you want?"

"No." I shake my head. "I'll be fine after a couple of Tylenol and a quick nap."

She reaches over again and tenderly kisses my cheek. "I'll get a cab home. Come over about eight o'clock and I'll cook. Just pasta, or something that I can't set fire to."

I chuckle and nod, quickly returning her kiss before she climbs out and shuts the door. I watch the sway of her delicious ass until she disappears into the building. Then I go home and fall into bed.

Thirty-Three

NOAH

SHE DOESN'T SEE ME. She's standing at the sink, rinsing some dishes with her Beats over her ears, and I growl under my breath the more her tight little ass swings to some music I can't hear.

Spinning round, she squeals and drops a mug. It doesn't break, just skittles across the floor and comes to rest by my feet.

"Jesus H Christ!" she exclaims. "You scared the crap out of me!"

She lifts a brow when I take a step towards her but remain silent. She's wearing a tight strappy top, the hemming embroidered with small, delicate flowers. It makes me want to laugh out loud. The whore should have toxic waste symbols weaving across instead of pale blue flowers.

She can feel my need as it pours from me and starts to overwhelm her. Her tongue pokes out and runs across her lips. She's hungry too.

She gasps when I grab her hair, fling her around and press her face into the wooden kitchen table. Her ass thrusts out of her short denim skirt when the position raises it, exposing the skimpiest thong I've ever seen. She has the most perfect ass. Well apart from Nina's. My dick hardens with the thoughts of that cute little cunt which had been mine for four whole hours.

Looking back down at my regular fuck, I slip my knife out of the waistband of my jeans. Her eyes widen as she looks over her shoulder at me.

"What are you . . . ?"

I grin.

"Noah?"

Her breathing has accelerated, her mouth dry as she recoats her lips. When she tries to stand I force her back down with the palm of my hand on the nape of her neck, then slip my knife under her top and slowly glide it up. The sharp blade slices through the material easily until the two halves of fabric part in the middle and fall each side of her. She is sans bra. My lip curls at the sight of her; her chest bare and a thong that's so tiny it doesn't cover anything.

"You're such a slut."

My words hit where I knew they would and her breath comes out in short, sharp gasps.

My knife snips the two strings of her 'underwear' and

the minute scrap of material falls to the floor around her feet. Her cunt is full and pink, the flesh soaked as she waits eagerly for my cock.

Leaning over her back, I slide my hand around the front of her neck and restrict her airway slightly. "Ask."

Her teeth run along her bottom lip and her pupils dilate. "Please," she whimpers. "Please give it me!"

Standing back up, I run my hands along her shoulders then down the center of her back, every ridge of her spine providing a course for my fingertips to follow. The deep press of my fingers leaves red streaks in a path down her pale skin.

She cries out when I thrust my cock inside her, right to the tip. Her back arches and the bitch practically sings my name in reverence.

I pull back out then slam back in—hard, hard enough that she cries out in pain when her ribs crush against the edge of the table. And again. And again. I know she's going to display bruises on her stomach for a while and my lips tilt at the thought.

"Fuck! Yes!" she shouts as I pummel her, my balls slapping against the top of her thighs as my fingers dig deep into her hips. She's always had a tight cunt, which surprises me being the whore that she is.

My eyes catch the knife that's resting on the table beside her and I pick it up, my hips still giving her a pasting. She shivers when she feels the steel of the blade on her skin, the tip trickling down her spine and producing a line of pure, red decoration. Tilting my head, I gaze at the trail and draw another one down the side of the first, another streak of crimson partnering its mirror image.

She squirms beneath me and lifts her head. "No."

"No?"

She looks scared when I dig the blade in deeper, her skin parting so beautifully that I only glance at her face for a fraction of a second, yet in that moment I can see her fear. But what she doesn't understand is that it only feeds me. It gives me more pleasure than her sanction ever could.

"NO?" I growl as I twist her hair in my fingers and hold her head rigid. "Never tell me no. Never!"

"Noah, please. You're hurting me."

Her whining is annoying me so I slip my fingers around her throat and tighten it until she can't get her vocal chords to work anymore. She's struggling underneath me, her body writhing the more I create a masterpiece on the blank canvas of her back.

My balls are screaming for release and it's only when she manages to scream around the compression of my fingers that I roar out my orgasm inside her, floods of my uniqueness filling her up until it trickles back down my balls and her tight thighs.

"What the fuck!" she pants, slapping at me when I draw out of her and refasten my fly. Her slaps are girly and weak. However, she stills when I grab the loose skin at the base of her throat and twist. Her face instantly turns white and her eyes begin to bulge.

"Now, now." I sigh in boredom. "Don't touch me again. You know the rules."

She splutters and her fingers come up to her throat instinctively when I let go. Her eyes brim with tears, a few drops too heavy to be contained as they spill down her red cheeks.

"I need to use your laptop. Go get it for me."

Her hurried pace feeds my ego. She's scared and finally realizing who she lets fuck her.

A while later, I smile and gently kiss her cheek. "Time's up. See you soon."

Then I leave, chuckling as I hear her sob of horror before I quietly close the door behind me, thinking about the email I sent Devon.

So it would appear cats really do have 9 lives

Shame Lady of the Lake didn't have.

Blood is so beautiful against snow white flesh

If you go down to the woods today you're sure to have a surprise.

Thirty-Four

Nina

"WHAT ARE YOU LAUGHING AT?" Luke asks Gerry, walking through from his office.

"That old lady, Miller, keeps calling about her cat whose been missing. She wants you to go out there." His eyebrows raise and he gives me a one sided smile.

"Don't you smirk at me, Sheriff Logan," I chastise in jest.

"What is it with women phoning the sheriff for missing cats?"

"Our pussies mean a lot to us."

Gerry's mouthful of coffee spurts out all over his desk

and he begins choking. My eyes revert back to Luke, who's shaking his head with a huge toothy grin spread across his face.

"And I take it very seriously, Miss Drake, because they mean a lot to me too, so I'm going to drive out there right now."

I think back over what I said and my eyes expand and my cheeks warm. "Oh, grow up, you two," I admonish, and we all break into a chorus of laughter. Luke disappears out the front door as Brady walks through it and I make myself busy with printing and filing the call reports.

I look up from my desk when two unfamiliar men in suits walk through the doors. Giving them a smile, I gesture with a finger that I'll be with them shortly. The tallest one returns my smile and nods.

"I'll get someone straight over, Mr. Hardy."

"Oh, you're such a sweet thing," Mr. Hardy says before he ends his call.

I turn to Brady and lift up the slip of paper. "Looks like Ted's cows escaped again. They have deposited . . . *a present* in Mr. Hardy's front yard."

Brady blows out a frustrated breath as he snatches up his jacket from the back of his chair. "I swear if that man doesn't fix that damn fence soon I'm gonna have his ass in for it."

I hide my smile when he huffs and storms out, then look over at the two gentlemen. "Can I help you?"

The tall one pulls out a badge from his inside pocket. "Frank Poleski, Custer County Sheriff."

"Idaho?" I question, wondering what the hell two

cops from there would want here in this small dead-end town. The way they stand shows how important they feel they are, and I blink at Gerry when he strolls over from his desk.

"Sergeant Gerry Everett. How can I help?"

"The Sheriff in?" The short one, Brendon Aisling, according to his badge, asks.

Gerry shakes his head. "He's out of town for the day." Frank nods then takes out a piece of paper from his inside pocket, and unfolds it. "We have two Mispers. Sarah Reynolds and boyfriend, Sean Keller. Came out here fifteen days ago on vacation. Never returned."

"Uh-huh," Gerry mumbles, taking the photo from him. Studying it, he shakes his head again. "Not come up here." He looks to me. "Nina can you run a check on those names please."

"They won't be in the system," Brendon cuts in, his gruff voice making me uneasy. "We already checked."

Gerry quirks a brow at him. "Well, no harm done if we check again, is there?"

Before they start drawing out dicks to see whose is bigger, I log in and enter the missing couple's details. "Nothing on file," I tell them all.

Frank nods. "Well, if you can put out an alert to all your officers."

Gerry snorts, knowing there's only the three of them, but nods. "Of course. But you know, you could have just faxed the spec over."

"Wanted to take a look around," Frank mutters as his eyes scope out our small department. His lip curls slightly as if he is disgusted with what he's seeing, and I can't help but feel a bit offended, even if I have only worked here a short time. "Anyway." He thrusts a few flyers at me with the couple's photos and details on. "If you can be a doll and circulate these."

I catch Gerry tense beside me. Even he's taken a dislike to the egotistical manner in which he conducts himself. "Her name is Nina, and she will be happy to do almost anything for you if it's accompanied with a please."

Frank's eyes widen on Gerry, who glares back. I smile inwardly at Gerry's back-up when he takes a protective step towards me and rests his hand on my shoulder.

Quickly butting in to avoid a war, I force a smile at Frank and his crony. "I'll make sure these are situated in every establishment in the area, sir. If you could be so kind as to email us the case specifics," I tell him, jotting down the office email address and handing it to him. "And I'll be sure to alert your office should we receive any response."

He drops his eyes from Gerry to me and covers his face with a sickly smile. He doesn't thank me, just nods once before turning and leaving with his shadow in tow.

"City pricks," Gerry utters as we watch them get into their car and pull off the lot.

I can't help but chuckle to myself when, as though answering all the evils of the world, Gerry snaps open a variety Dunkin' Donuts box and takes a bite out of a sugarcoated one. "They need to learn to chill the hell out!" he grumbles to himself.

"And eat a donut," I whisper.

The lasagna is baking in the oven, the salad and bread is prepared, and the wine is chilling in the fridge. The table is laid with a thin white lace cloth and pink candles, and I've created a short playlist of love songs ready to go on Spotify. I'm not sure why, but I want to make an effort tonight. So, forgoing my usual jeans and tee for a knee length, rose-colored skirt and a floaty cream blouse, I also trade my usual cotton briefs and bra for new lacy underwear and an all-over wax. I smile to myself as I add a layer of sheer gloss to my lips and some mascara to highlight my lashes.

It's not often I wear cosmetics, even at work. I find it intimidating, like it's inviting a man to look at me, as though I'm dressing myself for him. However, tonight I want to look nice for Devon. I know he thinks me... *pretty* without it, but a little help never goes amiss.

Nodding to myself in the mirror, pleased with what looks back at me, I reach for my favorite perfume. I frown when it isn't on my dresser, and pull the dresser from the wall slightly to see if it's fallen behind.

"Huh?" I purse my lips, thinking where it could be. *Bathroom—where you last used it.* I search the small space but neither is it in the bathroom cabinet or set on the vanity. Before I can give it another thought, the doorbell rings and my heart flutters with excitement.

Slipping my heels on, I practically run down the stairs two at a time, but when I fling open the door, instead of Devon, Luke is standing on the porch.

"Oh."

He lifts a brow. "I know I'm not the pizza guy, but I did expect a warmer welcome."

I laugh and shake my head. "I'm sorry. I was expecting someone else."

His eyes slowly roam over me and his brow puckers slightly when they reach back up to my face. "So I see."

I blink at his strange reaction then shake it off and open the door wider. "I'm sorry, I'm being rude. Come in."

Accepting my offer, he steps into the hallway. His head rotates towards the kitchen and when he spots the decorated table he looks at me. "I apologize. You're busy."

"Oh, no. It's okay. Would you like a drink?"

He regards me for a moment then nods. "That would be good. Thank you."

"Wine, coffee . . . ?" I ask as he follows me through to the kitchen.

"Just water, thanks."

He looks uncomfortable as he takes the glass from me. "Is it okay if we sit?"

I frown, suddenly anxious from the tone of his voice and the expression that's troubling his usually strong features. "Sure." I nod then take a seat opposite him.

Placing his glass on the table, he takes a deep breath and clears his throat. "So, you know I was going back to Kansas to visit your neighbor?"

"Yes."

He grasps at his forehead with exasperation and pauses, sighs and looks back at me. "It would appear Mr. Ilavich never moved out."

My eyes widen with hope and I smile at him. "Oh, that's good, isn't it? Maybe he saw something . . ."

"Nina," Luke halts me, his hand covering mine on the table. "I found Mr. Ilavich's body in his basement."

"What?" I stutter, pulling back and knocking the glass over. I quickly grab a towel to mop up the mess but Luke grips my arm and tells me to sit down. I take in a deep breath and nod, assuring him that I'm okay.

"The basement? What was he doing down there?" It's a stupid question because I already know the answer, but my mind is a little slow on the uptake; a lot slower than the vomit stirring in my belly.

"It looks like he's been dead a long time. Probably since the night of your attack going by the extensive decomposed state of his body."

"Oh my God." My hand slaps over my mouth involuntarily, and a small whimper climbs up my throat. "But, Teddy, his Chihuahua . . . surely he would have alerted someone . . . ?"

"I'm afraid his dog was also found at the scene."

I rush over to the sink when the vomit refuses to be confined to the tightness of my stomach, and bend over, throwing my guts up. Luke appears behind me, sweeping my hair into a bunch in his hand. His other hand settles on my back and strokes up and down smoothly when a sob wrenches from me. "It's okay, Nina," he soothes when I heave again. "I'm going to get this bastard. I promise."

"What the hell is going on?" I hear Devon's angry shout and turn just in time to see him pull Luke off me and floor him in one single punch.

Thirty-Five

Devon

THE BASTARD GOES DOWN IN one hit. I want to tear him to bits for touching what's mine. How dare he? How fucking dare he?

"Devon!"

Nina's soft fingers wrap around my forearm but I can't look away from the asshole on the floor as he rolls over and stares up at me, his hand cradling his chin.

"What the fuck?"

"Devon," Nina tries again. "What are you doing?"

Turning to her, I stare at her in confusion. "He was hurting you!"

Her face crumples for a moment but she shakes her head. "No, he wasn't. I was being sick. Sheriff Logan was holding my hair out of the way."

Sheriff Logan?

I look from Nina back to the Sheriff when he climbs

up off the floor. Fuck! I have completely fucked up.

"And you are?" he practically growls.

"Devon Trent, Nina's boyfriend."

He lifts both brows and looks at Nina. "Is this true?"

I'm a bit pissed that the bloke she works for hasn't a clue that Nina is in a relationship. That means that she hasn't mentioned me at work.

She nods quickly. "Yes." She looks between us both her eyes wide appearing anxious but steps towards me. "I'm sorry, Luke . . ." *Luke?* "Devon is very . . . protective." The way she smiles at me dampens my anger and I reach out and touch her chin.

"That's because you're worth protecting."

I forget the Sheriff is here, but I drop my hand when he coughs. He's studying me, but I suppose with his job, he studies everyone so I don't get too hyped up about it.

"You live where, Devon?"

I point out of the kitchen window. "Next door."

He turns to look where I'm pointing and nods. "Right. And how long have you lived there? I didn't realize Mr. Brochovich had passed."

"A few months."

He's contemplative, his brow furrowed deeply. I shiver. It feels like he can see straight through to my soul, but eventually he snaps out of it and looks back at Nina. "I'll leave you to enjoy your night and we'll talk tomorrow."

She nods and smiles. "Okay. Thanks, Luke."

He smiles at her and gives me a polite nod before letting himself out. Nina is looking at me with wide eyes but the way she's sucking on her lip, I know she's amused. "I can't believe you did that." She laughs. "You just laid out a cop!"

"I didn't know he was the law! It looked like he was trying to force your face through the waste disposal." I reach out and take her hand in mine when I see how pale she is. "Are you okay? You said you were being sick."

She nods and sighs. "Yeah. Luke went out to my old house." My body tenses and I struggle to hide it from her but she seems to miss it because she carries on. "He found my old neighbor dead in his basement."

"What?"

She blinks at the tone of my voice. This is news to me. What the hell is wrong with Noah? He has taken so many risks, and to kill the neighbor was stupid.

"Yeah. I mean, he wasn't very nice but he didn't deserve that."

She shudders, and I place my arm around her shoulders and pull her in for a hug. Her sobs are heavy and relentless, and she clings to me as though I can save her from the hell Noah put her in. I'm glad I'm no longer involved with him. He's a monster. The evidence of what's inside him is displayed so horrifically over every inch of Nina's skin, the mental scars too severe for her to show.

"I'm sorry, Nina. I'm so sorry."

She shakes her head and looks up at me, her red eyes full of a gentleness I have never witnessed in another person. Reaching up, she places her palm softly on my cheek. "Don't be sorry, Devon. You have nothing to be sorry for. You've helped me so much. You could never understand how much."

"But I haven't done anything."

Smiling, she kisses my jaw. "You have made me feel

like a woman again. A desired woman, a beautiful woman. And that was something I never expected to feel again. You've given me confidence. Believe it or not, since you moved here, my life has leapt forward. Before, I wouldn't even leave the house, yet now, I have a boyfriend, a job, and more than that, I have hope for the future."

Sliding my hands through her soft waves, I touch the tip of my nose to hers. "A future with me in it, I hope."

"I hope so too," she whispers as she rises onto her tiptoes and her full lips press against mine. I want to sigh in satisfaction, my whole body roaring with life just from the feel of her in my arms.

Her beautiful wide eyes blink at me and her hands slowly slide down the front of my shirt. When she reaches the waistband of my pants, her fingers fumble with my belt.

"I want to taste you," she whispers as she unbuttons and pulls down my fly then takes my hard cock in her fist. Her lips are burning a trail down my throat, and when she reaches the opening of my shirt, she slowly lowers herself to her knees before me. Her warm lips slip over the head of my cock and I hold back a groan. I try to take my mind elsewhere so I don't come in seconds but her lusty pulls keep me devoted to the moment when her greedy mouth slurps over me like I'm her favorite flavor lollipop. She drags me in deeper until the tip of my throbbing cock hits the back of her throat. Her hand grasps my balls and gently massages them. Her suction increases and she's swirling her tongue over the tip with every up pull. She's making desperate little moans over me and it's causing vibrations over the sensitive tip.

I grasp a handful of her hair for leverage, to stop myself from falling to my knees with pleasure when she speeds up the motion, taking me all the way down her throat. The hot flood of sensation races up my spine as my balls draw tight and my cum spurts out in the back of her throat.

"Oh, fuck!"

It's nice lying in her bed and settling down for the night. This is the closest I've ever felt to normal. Her supple little body pushes into mine and I sigh in contentment.

My phone pings with a new email. It's just a generic junk email that's been flagged by the protocols I have set up for my emails, but I notice one unopened from an unknown address.

> **So it would appear cats really do have 9 lives**
>
> **Shame Lady of the Lake doesn't have.**
>
> **Blood is so beautiful against snow white flesh**
>
> **If you go down to the woods today you're sure to have a surprise.**

I know it's from Noah but the email address is new and something I need to investigate but I can't from my cell. I need my laptop. What does he even mean with his riddles? I'm getting sick of his games. I'm not one of his marks, a plan for him to play. This had to end. Tomorrow I'll trace this IP address and go confront him once and for all.

Nina has fallen asleep, and before I know it my eyes are drooping too.

Thirty-Six

Nina

I'M FREEZING. THE COLD AIR on my feet makes my bladder twinge with need to empty. I hate when that happens and you can't sleep through the need. I groan and sit up, noticing the reason I'm cold is because my bed covers are in the middle of the room. *What the hell?* I reach behind me to shake Devon but my touch is met with a cold mattress. I stand and survey the room but he's not here. Maybe he went home . . . ?

The window is open and a steady breeze blows the curtains up into the air. No wonder I'm chilly. I cross the room, reach up to close the window, and startle when I see a silhouette of a man standing in the middle of the road, staring up at me. My heart stampedes in my chest and tears brim my eyes before I can think rationally. It's only when a car passes and blares its horn that he looks away. The headlights light up his body, identifying him to my eyes. Devon?

I rush from the room and down the stairs, bursting out the front door. The gravel cuts into the bottom of my bare feet and the chill in the air whips at my exposed arms.

"Devon?" I shake his arm and cup his cheek with my other hand, bringing his eyes down to mine. "Devon."

His pupils are huge and a grimace twists his beautiful features. My hand reacts on instinct and I slap him. I've been told never to wake a sleepwalker but damn that, he's shitting the life out of me and he might die if I leave him on the road until he wakes up from wherever he is.

His eyes blink open and closed, and his pupils dilate. "Nina?"

I let out a breath and grab his wrist to drag him inside.

"What's going on?" he asks, once inside.

"You were sleepwalking or something. What do you remember?" He looks down to the floor and then back up at me, pain slicing across his brow and causing his eyes to droop. His head shakes. "Fire and Noah."

He drops, defeated, into a chair, accidentally knocking my work bag to the floor. He jumps from the noise it makes.

He carries a burden, his dreams so intense that they cause a physical reaction. Mine are bad and I know what stalks me in my dreams. I wonder if Heather can help him or give me some advice on getting him to open up about what troubles his sleeping hours.

"What's this?" he asks, leaning down and picking up the picture of the two missing people. I don't answer straight away. I'm too confused about the way he's looking so intently at the images with his brow furrowed.

"They're missing."

He looks up briefly and then back down, stroking his finger over the image of the girl.

"Devon, do you know her?"

He drops the picture like it's lit on fire. "What? No, of course not. Why would you think that?"

"Just your reaction to her, is all. Are you okay? Do you always sleep walk?"

He screws his face up in distaste. "I don't sleepwalk! What's with all the questions?"

I hold up my hands. "Devon, what the hell? Calm down."

"I am calm, Nina. I need to go." He storms out, leaving the door open. Am I dreaming or is this really happening? And if so, what the actual hell?

I chase after him, not satisfied with how things played out. He's acting weird and I want to know why. I want to help ease any burden or nightmares he's clinging on to.

I find the downstairs empty so I go up into his bedroom. The bed is stripped bare and there's a huge blood stain in the middle.

"Why are you here?"

I jump out of my skin when he appears behind me. "Why are you acting this way? What have I done to warrant you having an attitude with me?" His eyes bore into me and I squirm under their scrutiny. "Devon, why is there blood on the mattress?" I ask timidly.

He looks over at the mattress and laughs without humor. He holds his palm up to my face. "My injury, Nina. Now, get out. I've had enough of your questions for one night."

I leave, completely devastated by the way he just behaved. Was I wrong to ask questions? I need to speak to someone. I've spent too long out of the dating game. I need to open up to Tricia and ask her advice on his behavior.

Thirty-Seven

Devon

I LOST CONTROL OF EVERYTHING last night. And I'm angry, at him, at myself.

Noah is inside my head, playing games and drawing out the other Devon, the one who gave up the life he desperately wants me to come back to. The Devon that he used, and in some ways, abused. This is what all his little games are about, to teach me a lesson. What it's like being on the outside of things.

I hadn't understood his 'lady of the lake' or 'go down to the woods' reference until I saw the missing person's poster from Nina's purse.

I rushed home to open the Snow White file I'd created on my computer from the images I captured the day of the lake, and sure enough it's her. The file had been corrupted and copied. *Fuck you, Noah!*

Then I caught Nina in my room and she questioned

the blood. My head was buzzing and I treated her like shit. I fucking hate myself right now for that; the image of her hurt is on replay in my mind, but I need her angry at me for a little while to keep her out of the way while I try to find Noah.

However, first, I need to go back to the lake where I know he's left me a gift.

Thirty-Eight

Nina

I SHARPEN ANOTHER PENCIL AND pop it in the cup holder. The day has been too quiet at work and it's not what I need. I need a busy day to keep me occupied. I think back over my call with Tricia last night. I'd woken her and she was grouchy. When I told her about mine and Devon's relationship she was surprised, despite admitting she thought he liked me when she stayed, but the more I went into detail about how amazing things had been, the more dismissive she became, and if I'm being honest with myself, she sounded jealous. Really horribly jealous. It wasn't like her. She's known for her bitchy comments but not bitterness. It hurt to hear it in her tone.

"Stop complaining that he asked you to leave when you probed him with questions. You're so pathetic when it comes to men, Nina. Yet they all trip over themselves to try and be with you."

At that point I told her to go back to sleep because she was being a bitch and hung up. I was feeling out of sorts. Had I woken up in an alternative reality where everyone I loved had turned into an asshole?

"I think we have enough pencils." I look up at Luke who's holding my hand still over the sharpener. He cocks a brow at the cup containing way too many sharp, pointy pencils. "What's eating you?"

I roll my eyes. "Maybe the fact you told me my old pervy neighbor was murdered along with his poor ankle biting dog." I sigh and smile when he squeezes my hand. "It's because he saw something isn't it? He was killed because of me."

"It's likely that's what happened, yes. But that still doesn't make it your fault. You were a victim too, Nina."

His eyes hold such sadness for me that it almost makes me want to comfort him. How crazy is that?

"Why didn't he kill me?" It's a question I've always asked myself.

"Someone as depraved as him? I suppose he gets off on it, letting the victim live. It's something he chose to do which, in his mind, gives him power. Makes him feel like God. His choice as to whether you live or die. It's also harder to survive those kinds of assaults for some women than to not. You don't even know how strong and amazing you are, do you?" He smiles and it reaches his eyes.

"I don't feel amazing."

"What's really bothering you? You were happy yesterday. Tell me more about this Devon guy. How long have you known him?"

I smile to myself, then last night's weirdness comes back and my smile falters. "He moved in around five months ago but we've only been in a relationship for around two of those. Although I've gotten to know him over the five months he's been here he's still very . . . closed off. I'm just a bit . . . I don't know really, I found him sleepwalking last night and he got really defensive when I tried to help him."

Luke frowns but doesn't voice what's on his mind. "I noticed his hand was bandaged. Did he do that during one of his episodes?"

"Oh no, that was an accident with his back window. He got it stitched and it's fine."

Luke's cell rings and he rolls his eyes as he pulls it from his pocket. "No rest for the wicked."

"If it's Mrs. Perry, I'm not here!"

He laughs. "You spoilsport. The woman is lonely." He laughs as he answers his phone. He listens for a while then looks at me with an amused expression causing me to frown. "And when did you last see your cat, Mrs. Miller?"

I poke my tongue out at him and mouth, "See? Now there's more crazies than me in town."

He chuckles quietly and nods then turns. I watch him walk away, the muscles on his broad back tight against the material of his shirt. I've settled in perfectly, and I'm proud of myself, I've made friends and have a job I love. And of course, Devon. Although he was short with me last night, I knew he was just feeling a little run down. He'd been tired and, his migraine probably affected him more than he'd let on.

The desk phone rings and I peer hesitantly at the display, "Damn it!" Blowing out a breath, I pick it up. "Good morning, Mrs. Perry. How can I help you today?"

Thirty-Nine

Devon

THE LAKE IS QUIET WHEN I slip through the gap in the bush at the south end of the grounds. It's early afternoon and I'm lucky to find it deserted. I'm nervous as I venture further in. Before, a year ago, I would have been bouncing with anticipation as I clutched my camera hungrily, Noah's games making me salivate, but now I don't want this shit. I want the life that most people have; go to work, come home for an evening with the family and then to bed again, work, home and bed. It's maybe boring to some, but after the whole of my life has been full of cruelty and depravity, I crave boring.

The wind picks up as I step into the open area and stirs the dead leaves around my feet, the breeze rustling whatever leaves remain on the trees above and around me. It's almost too quiet and my body shudders apprehensively.

My gaze settles across the water to where I last saw the

young couple swimming and having sex. I can still picture them, their bodies molded together in their moment of passion.

I take another look around. Noah must have been watching that day, watching me take shots of the amorous twosome. He isn't here now. I'm not sure how I'm positive about that, just that I am.

I slowly make my way around the lake, my eyes flicking everywhere. My feet shuffle because I know what I'm going to find and I don't want to. I don't want to see what my brother is capable of yet again.

This to him is a sport, amusement to stop him being bored, and now that I'm included in the game, a pawn in his sick and twisted recreation, his competitive streak will be at full strength, his need to show me who is boss driving him harder and harder.

I'm worried for Nina, yet for some reason I know she will be the last move of the board for him. I come first. It isn't about Nina anymore, this is about us; me and my brother.

A noise to my left makes me stop and tilt my head to the side. I frown, cussing the wind when it hinders my hearing. I turn towards the wooded area it came from and walk slowly forwards, my throat aching when it starts to constrict with unease. I know as soon as I see the faint smear of blood on a rock that's sat under a tree that they are here, and I'm on the right route Noah has mapped out for me. Glancing down at the stone, I ignore the need to reach down and wipe at the blood with my fingers. The last thing I should do is leave any of my own DNA at the scene.

My heart beats out of my chest when I hear a quiet whimper from further into the wooded area. They're here, there's no doubt about it. Another low sob makes my feet move again and I move branch after branch out of my way as I stagger into the dense forest.

I close my eyes and take a fortifying breath when I spot a pair of shoes poking out from behind a bush. My mouth dries and my stomach twists as I make my way around.

"Jesus fucking Christ!" I choke out when the scene unfolds. The guy's naked body is propped up against a tree in a sitting position. He has a wreath made of twigs around his head, the sharp thorny parts embedded in his skull. His only hand is in his lap and in his hand is his . . . head. His eyes are still wide open, as wide open as his mouth is in his silent scream. Snow White is laid on her back in front of him, her Prince's severed arm protruding from her cunt, her legs wide when she appears to have two broken hips. Her long black hair is spread like a halo around her head and her dislocated jaw holds a bright red apple. And even after all that, the thing that sickens me the most is the seven large stones that circle her. Each one has a comical face drawn on it, each posing a different face. It's obvious they are the seven dwarves.

"IT'S JUST A GAME TO YOU, ISN'T IT?" I scream, spinning in a circle when my anger guts me. But I'm more angry at myself when my thoughts linger to my camera and how much fun I would have had documenting this scene.

"WHAT DO YOU WANT? WHAT THE FUCK DO YOU WANT FROM ME?"

I gasp when Snow White whimpers. I look at her in shock, amazed when I find her eyes on me. "I can't help you!" Her eyes widen and she sobs again. "I can't!"

Closing my eyes, I shake my head again, then turn and leave. I know she'll be dead soon. She won't be able to tell anyone I was there. But I can't risk leaving any scent of me around them. I just can't, as monstrous as that makes me. Their fairy-tale is ending, yet mine, with Nina, is just beginning and I won't risk that for anyone.

My body is exhausted as I pull up on my driveway. I have another migraine coming and I need to take some painkillers and crash before it becomes unbearable.

Steve meanders over when I climb from my car and twists his fat little body around my feet. "Gimme a chance, big guy," I murmur as I flick the locks on the car and walk up the side of the house to the side entrance. My feet stumble when the fucking Sheriff appears from the back of the house.

His eyes narrow and I swear he hears me growl in irritation. "Mr. Trent," he says. "Sorry to trouble you. I wondered if I can have a quick word."

My teeth virtually vibrate in my mouth but I force a smile. "Of course." Unlocking the door, I gesture for him to come inside. He follows me, and when I turnaround, his eyes are everywhere, scrutinizing my things, my life. "What can I do for you?"

"Well, nothing really. I came to start again."

I frown, my body stiffening. "I'm sorry, I'm not with you."

"Yesterday." He smiles. "Our little altercation. I didn't want you worrying that I'm going to press charges against you."

I hadn't given it another thought but I smile. "I appreciate it. Thank you."

He nods. "It seems that Nina is important to us both and I didn't want any hard feelings between us to make her feel awkward."

I tip my head, my heart rate escalating as I stare him out. His lips twitch as if he's aware what's racing through my mind. It isn't hard to interpret what he's really saying. He fancies his own chances with her? The fucker thinks he is in with a chance to slip into her little cunt. That he can easily take her from me?

Not a fucking hope in hell.

"I see you're good with cats." He nods down at Steve who is still weaving his way through my legs. "Do you find they always gravitate towards you?"

What sort of question is that? I don't answer him, regarding him with narrow eyes.

"So, where are from originally, Devon?"

"What the fuck is this?" I snap. "Am I a suspect in some stupid investigation?"

He stares at me, my outburst stunning him but he slowly shakes his head. "Well, of course not. Unless there's something I need to know about you."

"What the fuck?"

He holds up his hands in defense. "I apologize. I was

joking, but it would seem we have a different sense of humor."

I grit my teeth, squeezing my bottom lip with my top teeth. "Yes, it looks that way."

He gives me a smile, one that causes his eyes to glint, but then his grin breaks and he coughs, rubbing at his chest. "Can I trouble you for a glass of water?"

Does this look like a diner? I stomp over to the sink and run him a glass of lukewarm water just to be an asshole. Handing it to him, I quirk a brow, silently asking if he's done but he grimaces. "Can I be a real pain and ask for some ice. It's so hot today."

Huffing, I snatch open the freezer and grab a couple of cubes then turn and virtually throw them in his glass. "We done?"

He chuckles and places the full glass down on the counter without even touching the damn thing after the run-around he's given me over it. "I'll be off then. I just thought we should clear the air. Have a good day, and thanks for the water."

He lets himself out as I stand rooted to the spot in the kitchen. "For fuck's sake, Steve!" I snarl as I grab his food and scoop some onto his saucer, my temper still bubbling away inside me.

"Motherfucker needs to back the fuck off," I murmur before my head starts to throb with pain. "Fuck!" I grate out, stumbling into the hallway and up the stairs to my bedroom.

The laptop is still open on the bed and I sit down, bringing up the email from Noah again. I blink and peer closer. This time the idiot has fucked up. It's got a traceable

IP address because the program I ran before I went out has come up with a hit.

"Got you."

Clicking the details tab, my mouth falls open at the name and address.

"Holy shit! No."

IP: 6.12.143.901
Address. 4513 Franklin Boulevard
Kansas
Registered to: Tricia Bentley.

Forty

NOAH

I DON'T USUALLY CARE OR ask why a client wants a job done, but ever since Devon decided we weren't playing by the normal rules anymore I became just as intrigued with pretty little Nina as he did, the difference being I know who wanted the assault to happen to her, just not why. This client, like all of them, was a referral from a rich bastard who earned his fortune in the underground fighting trade. He vouched for her, and the plan was made via calls and bank transfer of funds. She hadn't wanted a meet or to be involved, but I wanted to meet her. I had been strangely intrigued by her. My usual clients are male.

I look up at the client and my fuck buddy hanging from the chain she let me install in her room for kinky sex. My mind goes back to the first night I met and fucked her.

"Another!" I demand from the cocky guy behind the bar. He glares at me and I smirk in return.

He shouts down the bar for a waitress, Tricia. Her ass is showing out of the bottom of her too short jean skirt, and her top shows off more tit than fabric.

"Well, hello." She laughs, looking around me to see if I'm alone.

"Yeah, there's no girlfriend sweetheart." I grin and she quirks a brow.

"Is that right?"

I tap my glass, letting her know to refill it. "And have one for yourself." She's studying me, trying to figure me out, which is usually my job. "I'm Noah and I'll be fucking you later." I cut to the chase. I don't have time for her shit. I have plans to play out and a brother to claim back.

She chokes on the spit filling her mouth. I know she wants me. I'm easy on the eyes. "So, we're really doing this?" she asks. I knock the drink back she's poured and order her to get her coat. "Todd, I need to leave early."

"Tricia, are you fucking kidding me right now? You don't even know him and you're supposed to be at mine tonight."

She lifts a shoulder and smirks back at him. "I do know him." She looks over at me and then back to him. "He's Noah." She makes air quotes with her fingers and saunters over to me.

I throw her over my shoulder and slap her ass. She

screeches, and that's the first of many for her tonight. I flip Todd the middle finger and march from the bar. "Are you into role play, Tricia?"

"Are you?" She laughs so I smack her across the top of the thighs, hard enough to make my palm sting and for her to gasp in pain.

"When I'm fucking you, you'll be your little best friend, Nina Drake."

"Of course I will." She huffs. "And you'll be?"

"I'm just Noah. Always Noah."

I can smell her blood as it disperses into the air and makes me shiver with pleasure. I'll leave the questions for Devon to ask. Just to see if it's enough to get him to kill . . . again.

Things are coming to a head and the end is in sight. My world has become too distorted without Devon on my side. I lose time and sleep, and the gratification in new marks isn't the same without him. I'm not me without him . . . I need him back.

Forty-One

Nina

I'M TYPING UP SOME CASE files when Luke walks through the glass doors after going to investigate a call he'd received from a crazy woman about a dead body she'd found while out walking her dog. He'd found it amusing, saying that the only thing that gets killed around here is the local wildlife by Travis Greaves' tractor when it manages to get over the speed of 16 KPH. But as he'd said, it's his job to follow it up.

I look up and frown at his pale face. "Are you okay?"

For a moment he doesn't say anything, but then his eyes close slowly and he shakes his head before reopening them and sighing loudly. "In all my years doing this damn job I've never witnessed something so . . ." He doesn't finish but he blows out a breath when he gags.

He looks at me, and the horror in his eyes leaves me unable to move. "Luke?"

"You better get on to the guys from Idaho. I just found their Mispers."

"Oh no." My voice is quiet, my stomach twisting. It's obvious from Luke's expression that he didn't find them alive but I have to verify what I need to tell the Custer Sheriff's department. "Are they . . . dead?"

He nods. "Yeah, forensics are with them now. I pulled a partial print from a locket she was wearing," He sighs again and swallows. "Those poor kids. I don't envy Custer having to tell the families. They were no more than eighteen, Nina. What kind of fucking . . . monster . . ."

He doesn't finish. Shaking his head, he walks across the room and enters his office, slamming the door behind him. I turn to watch him, viewing him through the blinds when he opens the top drawer of his desk and pulls out a bottle of whisky, then without pouring a glass, he puts the bottle to his lips and slugs down a good mouthful. Wiping his mouth with the back of his hand, he suddenly turns and vomits into the wastepaper basket.

My heart goes out to him. I couldn't do his job for any amount of money. I know the scene he found was a rough one, his revulsion telling me as much.

I pick up the phone and make the call to Sheriff Frank Poleski with a heavy heart.

Ten minutes later, I pop my head into Luke's office. "Custer will be another two hours."

He looks up at me from what he's doing on the computer and nods. "Okay. I have some stuff I want to check out so I'll be a while. You can go. I'll wait for them."

"You sure? I don't mind waiting."

Shaking his head, he smiles at me. "Go on, get yourself home."

"See you in the morning."

I know he's watching me leave. I can feel his eyes burning into my back as I check my cell for any calls or texts. I hadn't heard from Devon all day and after the incident last night, I'm getting a little worried.

I try calling him but it goes straight to voicemail and as I climb in my car, I try again.

"God damn it, Devon. Where are you?" I mumble as I sling my cell on the passenger seat and make my way home, my worry worsening the nearer I get.

His car isn't in his drive when I pull onto mine but his front door is wide open. Steve is rolling about on the front yard as I hesitantly push the door wider. Silence is all that greets me. "Devon?" I shout as I step inside.

Nothing seems out of order as I walk along the hallway, Steve now following me with loud meows. "Ssh," I order when I reach the basement door. It's always been closed every other time I've been here, yet this time it's open.

I shout Devon's name again as I start down the old stone steps, the wear in them the same as the ones at my house, and I grab hold of the rail to steady myself when my heels prove a problem.

As I step off the last stair, my eyes widen at the dim red room. It's a darkroom, for developing photos. Long trestle tables are lined up with trays of fluids and other equipment, and some photographs are developing on pegs hanging from lines of string.

I look over them, awed at how good a photographer Devon is. I move across them, smiling and examining each one. This truly is something that he obviously loves, the perfection to each image astounding. He seems to capture the life of each object, emotion pouring from every single picture. But then as I reach the end of one line I freeze. I blink, making sure I'm actually seeing what my brain tells me it sees.

"Oh my God."

I reach out, knowing I shouldn't touch developing pictures, but it's almost involuntary, my disbelief needing something physical to touch to make it real.

The two missing people, who are now dead, stare back through a variety of pictures. There's dozens of them, from them swimming in the lake to them messing around, and then some of them having sex. How could Devon spy on them, and take shots of such a private thing between two people? But more to the point, he had known who they were when he found the flyer in my purse. I asked him if he knew them and he point blank said no. I hadn't imagined or dreamed that he'd said no. It's there, clear as anything in my memory banks.

How could he lie to me? How could he document the moments before their death and hide it? This could be huge to Luke's case, evidence of what the poor young couple were doing right before someone murdered them.

I snatch a couple down, hating that I'm betraying Devon, but this is so wrong. As I turn to leave, another string of images comes into view. My heart stops, its stutter making my legs weak. I can't seem to breathe properly as each photograph blinds me. They're of me. Me in my bedroom, in the garden, in my car, behind my desk at work through the front window of the department.

"What the ... ?"

They're all candid shots, pictures I wasn't aware of him taking. Some people would be honored to be 'idolized' like this, but I'm not. I'm sickened by it. It's as though he was watching me, stalking me even. He'd told me that he wanted to photograph me but I thought he meant posed shots, ones I had given my permission for. This is wrong. So wrong.

I stumble when I start to flee the room, sickened by it all, my foot kicking a box that's pushed under the table. Bending to make sure I haven't broken anything, I frown when I see it contains dozens of DVDs, all with numbers and names on. My eyes widen on one.

Nina Francis Drake
Client: 1325

A shiver tears up my spine. My instincts are hyper, and my skin prickles with goose bumps when my mind tells me Devon is hiding something. Something big.

Snatching up the DVD, I race through the house, I shout for him once more and decide to check if he's up stairs. The place is quiet and empty but Devon's laptop is open on the bed. Checking the bathroom to assure myself he really isn't home I find myself hovering over his laptop. My palms are sweating as I move my finger across the touchpad to shift it out of standby mode. I'm panicking, my heart rate peaking as I listen for Devon's car pulling up the drive. I feel wrong snooping but then I tell myself that Devon has been doing the very same thing to me, going as far as catching me in frames as he spies on me.

When the Windows desktop loads up, I scan across the various files. 'CamFeed' jumps out at me and I open the program.

"Oh—my—fucking—God."

I never cuss yet 'Fuck' doesn't even seem harsh enough when a view of each room in my house pops up. He's been watching me, viewing everything I do. The bile in my gut burns when I spot one of the feeds in my bathroom. The dirty bastard! Tears scorch my retinas, each one a piece of my soul as it disintegrates inside me. How could he?

Picking up the laptop, I throw it across the room. I don't care that he'll find it. I smash my hand across his dresser, his stupid colognes scuttling across the floor, followed by his clothes when I tear each drawer from its housing and rip his bedroom apart.

How could I have been so stupid? I've fallen in love with him. He allowed me to fall in love with him. He worked me, and like the stupid girl I am, I fell for him. The pain in my heart is intolerable, its shatter creating huge heaving sobs as I burst out of his house and into my own.

Slumping on the sofa, I draw my knees up to my chest and cry. I thought he was someone special. His compassion and adoration seemed so genuine. Yet it has all been a lie. He's a pervert and he played me until I practically fell at his feet and begged him to fuck me.

The DVD burns a hole in my hand as I spin it in my

fingers, then sliding off the sofa, I insert this disc into the machine and press play.

Forty-Two

Devon

WALKING UP THE SIDE OF the house to the back door, I sigh. I know he's expecting me. The note stuck to the door tells me how well my brother can read my every move.

The client who ordered your precious Nina's job awaits you, brother.

Client? What does that mean? It hits me all at once, and I have to grab the doorframe to stop the shake in my legs, sending me to ground. Tricia had been the one who ordered the hit on Nina.

"Holy shit!"

Knowing the door will be unlocked, I push it open and step inside. It's eerily quiet. As if I can smell the scent of corruption and sin, I instinctively make my way up the stairs. For some reason, I'm not apprehensive. I even reach into my bag and take out my camera. She feels heavy in my hand, but so right. So perfect, like her weight is the very thing that regulates every beat of my heart.

I had sworn that never again would I capture anyone's pain and misery, or their last breaths. But today, I know I will once more dip into the realms of hell. A hell I was born to. A hell that rules every one of my cells.

Tricia slowly tilts her head as I walk into the bedroom. She struggles and it's gratifying to witness. Her demise, the state she's in.

Lifting my camera, I sigh as bliss slithers through my veins. Everything once again right with the world as my blood flows freer and the oxygen in the air seems easier to breathe.

I followed the crimson river flowing down between her pert breasts through the lens; the deep rouge substance slowly travelling over the deep ridges of her breastbone, a pattern developing in the path of blood and leading her life force to pool on the floor around her tiny soft feet, her toes squelching in the puddle.

Click.

Capturing her death was the embodiment of power; watching her dreams leave her so unreservedly and so effortlessly. Witnessing her once strong will desert her and mock her bitterly was rather sad to watch, a void now occupying where fullness had once influenced. If we never had anything to rely on but our commitment to oneself then what had we actually ever had? This girl had been taunted by her mother's condemnations her whole life, and outcast because she didn't surpass her mother's ideals for a daughter. As she swayed before me, her forced splendor now of no support or comfort, then all she had strived for was an irrelevance blown away by the breeze of her final breath.

Click.

Her faint murmured moan brought a smile to my lips, the sound as empowering as seeing the blood now trickle over the small swell of her stomach, her pale skin alive with the adornment of the deep color, her character escaping with each traitorous pump of her heart.

Click.

The heart was such a deceitful thing. She thought she had loved, and had been loved. This small, frail life before me never collected anything but false genuineness all her tragic life. But all she had witnessed was a deception of hope, her mind manipulating every emotion that had been given to her. There was nothing real in emotion. The only genuine thing she would feel was the slowing of her heart and the light fading in her mind. Was it all worth it?

Click.

Her chest stuttered for a moment, encouraging me to click quickly and rapidly, my need to take her final gasp prisoner in the lens a vital necessity. I owed her the idolization of life, her soul fossilized to allow her existence a memory.

Click, click, click.

She gasped, but it was too deep and strong to be the final one. This one was spirited, almost as if she refused to grant me my petition.

Click.

I was growing tired; such a long day. The bitter wind

blew through every available cavity in my space, making me shudder angrily, the hairs under my shirt shivering at the chill coming through the window.

Click.

I was surprised, my head tilting and my own eyes widening as hers slowly opened and she managed to focus on me. She frowned faintly, unnerved but surprised by my presence. "W . . . why?" she rasped, her cracked lips splitting and giving my camera more opportunity to work. They never spoke to me. Never. But she was different from them. Personal. I tipped my head, both stunned and humbled by her fight.

Click.

"Why?" she repeated, her voice quiet as her breathing slowed. Lowering the camera, I stared at her. Of course, she wouldn't understand. They never do. Not until the end.

"Because capturing the making of angels, light or dark, is sacred." She didn't scoff or stare at me. Instead, curiously, she nodded faintly.

"You . . . you should know . . ." Her mouth was unmoving as she pushed her vocal chords to do the work for her. " . . . I'm no angel. I have sinned, and as such there is nothing for me after death."

I smiled and stepped towards her. She didn't move back. The chain she hung from still allowed her a little movement. She was simply quite beautiful if her insides were not so ugly. This end for her was a good choice. After all, to her, it was all about appearance. Maybe all this would fill the hole inside her that caused her corruption. I hoped so, for her sake.

"And in the righteousness shall a seraph ripen to become a beast of the heaven." I mocked. There was no faith here, neither her nor my own. There was only life and death and I was here to enjoy hers.

She blinked at my words and as I lifted the lens to finally capture the death that encompassed her, she whispered back, "And in the beast shall an angel of virtuousness flourish. I forgive you."

Click.

"You can only forgive those that you know, those that you understand. You neither know me nor understand me."

Confusion distorts her features. "Of course, I know you." Her breathing labors to an almost wheeze as her last word pushes past her lips. "Noah."

Everything around me is thrown into chaos with that one single word; that name. My mind ruptures, splintering into jagged shards and piercing me with unwanted visions. I grab her face but the light is already distinguishing. "What did you call me?"

"Noah," she whispers as blood starts to trickle from the corner of her mouth. She can't die now, not yet.

"I'm not Noah. I'm Devon! Devon Trent!"

She hasn't even got the energy to fight me when my fist curls around her thin throat. "Why did you hurt Nina? Why did you ask Noah to hurt her?"

She chuckles, triggering her to cough and spit blood onto my face. "Always so perfect. And so effortlessly. Why should she have it all?" She starts to heave as she struggles against the fill of blood in her lungs. "Noah!" she cries out as her body convulses painfully.

"I AM NOT NOAH!"

"You will always be my Noah," she chokes out as my fingers around her throat tighten. Her eyes bulge before they seem to burst in her head and blood seeps from the edge. "I love you," she whispers, and then she is gone. And so am I.

The camera falls, cracking on the floor and shattering along with my grip on reality, my sanity dissolving.

My thoughts are wrong, disjointed. I feel like I'm tearing out of my skin and my psyche is splintering into thousands of tiny slivers. I can't switch off the pandemonium inside me. I can feel him inside me, screaming for release but it can't be true . . . I can't be him. How the fuck would that even be possible? Noah is my brother, the boy who took care of me when I was young, when I'd hurt myself. He'd been the one who held me and told me everything would be okay. He's real. He's a real person who breathed air through his lungs and saw the world through real eyes.

It's like I'm slipping away bit by bit, with no anchor to tell me it's okay and that she's lying, but a part of me knows there's something different about me lately. I've been losing time, memories, even objects . . . everything is hazy and then indistinct when I try to lock down specific times. My migraines have been getting worse and they've knocked me out for hours, sometimes days and I put the weirdness I'd been feeling down to them.

Leaping from the car, I rush through Nina's front door and the world fractures into particles of fire and internal chaos. I can't shut the noise out and I baulk as screams echo from the fire, hissing out and engulfing everything.

Then there's nothing.

"Devon, what is this?"

I look at the TV and tip my head in confusion. Then I turn to the tear-soaked face of Nina, the woman who caused all these truths to the surface, the woman I love but Noah hates.

How can I contain such strong, differing emotions? Intense, soul-consuming love and a deep seated hatred, within the same entity if I really am both me and Noah. Is this what it's like to be crazy? Or is this another play by Noah, and I'm tumbling down the rabbit hole he dug.

"Why would you have this?"

Nina's hysteria breaks my heart, her despair so potent that I struggle to swallow through the thickness of her emotions, her horror. How can I even explain any of this to her when I can't fathom the truth myself?

The sound from the television draws both our attention and that's when it dawns on me what she's watching—Noah's brutal attack.

My mouth opens but I can't force the words free. I'm struggling to breathe never mind talk. But just as I manage to croak out her name, the view on the TV rotates around a room, Nina's old bedroom, furniture whizzing past as though on a conveyer belt until Noah fills the screen.

"She was a fighter Devon," his eerie voice echoes through the speakers. The voice is deeper than my own. "I said you can have her but I didn't say in what condition." He pulls the balaclava from his head and the blood hurtling scream that tears from Nina's throat brings me to my knees. My face is filling the screen; *my* eyes, *my* lips, *my* chin, fuck even the mole under my right eye is taunting my sanity, ridiculing my every thought and memory.

How can this be real?

My mind snaps back to the fire, and Noah standing in front of me, asking what I had done, but the more I try to focus on him, his image warps like I'm looking at projection of him. He's distorted and muffled. Oh God, acceptance sinks in and I realize he wasn't there. He wasn't with me, next to me and talking to me. Had he been inside?

Burning? Dying?

Did I kill him?

Forty-Three

Nina

I'M VANISHING. EVERYTHING INSIDE ME is crumbling to dust as my soul drags my heart into despair. It can't be. How would I not know? How can they be the same person? Why would he do that to me?

The sob retching from my body is so intense it makes me vomit. My mind can't cope with the information it's being shown, and all I want to do is evaporate into the atmosphere and be nothing but a speck only seen when the sun streams through the window. My heart is in so much agony I can't contain the pain, and find myself clawing at my chest to try and rid me of the venom pumping inside.

How can I have let myself fall in love with him? He's

a monster and I let him into my life, my bed, my heart. I want to shower in acid to cleanse every single part of me. I've betrayed myself yet again and the realization of my foolishness is cruel and deep.

My head jerks in his direction when I notice he hasn't moved. My body reacts involuntarily and I charge him, screaming as all the memories attack my system like poison. "You son of a bitch! I hate you!" I slap at him but he doesn't move. There's nothing in his eyes, just a vacant abyss that chills me to the core of my very soul. "You killed Ginger! You killed my cat, you bastard. She was innocent! She did nothing to deserve that. I didn't deserve that. Argh!" I scream, pounding my tiny fists against his hard, stoic body.

Suddenly, with lightning speed, he grabs my wrist and backhands me across the face, sending me tumbling to the ground. A faint gasp leaves me although I don't know why I'm surprised. I know what he's capable of. I've been at the hand of his perversions before, in both reality and my nightmares but it still breaks whatever's left of my heart.

His head rolls along his shoulders and the grimace marring his face changes his features, almost altering his appearance. Gone is the man I fell for, and in his place, a beast.

"Well, well. Look what the cat dragged in," he mocks, looking down at me with amusement. "You look a little distraught, sweet Nina. Did Devon finally tell you about me? Or is it your best friend's betrayal that has you all misty-eyed? What a pathetic waste of life you are. Even your friends hate you."

He is crazy. It's like a completely new person is wearing Devon's face. Why is he speaking about himself in a third person, and what friend? He's completely insane. "What friend?" I ask as I try hopefully to stall him from advancing on me.

He laughs loud into the room but it's void of anything human, he's possessed by the devil himself.

"You really are fucking clueless about the monsters that surround you, Nina, aren't you?"

"Enlighten me then," I tell him in a shaky tone.

"I thought you'd had all the enlightening you could handle from me, Nina, but I'm sure after fucking my boring brother for a while you could use a good hard fucking."

"Don't you dare touch me, Devon! I swear to God, I'll kill you." I speak with a confidence I'm not sure I can follow through with, given his strength against mine but I know I'll never be his victim again. I'll bite my tongue off and drown in the blood before I let him take anything from me again.

"My name's Noah. Did I knock the sanity out of you?"

A hysterical laugh bubbles out of me; I can't help it, everything is shattering all rationality. He moves, stalking me with precise steps, and as I try to run, he kicks out with his foot. I put my hand out to protect my face and cry out when the bone in my finger makes a popping sound from the impact. It's broken, bent at an unnatural angle. I want to scream, I want to beg him to leave but my voice is stuck, strangled by my own fear.

"Don't mock me. I will gut you from throat to asshole and show you all the pretty inside."

My body tremors, the marrow in my bones vibrating with dread as his threat causes such intense fear I'm almost in disbelief that this is happening again. This can't be real, can it? I'm questioning my own sanity.

"I loved you, Devon. Why make me fall in love? Was that part of some twisted game?" I whisper, desperate for answers to sate the chaos in my head.

"You don't know me!" he screams as though his own lucidity is ripping from his very insides. "What are you talking about, and why are you calling me Devon? My name is Noah!"

Oh my God. He really believes that he is Noah. He's deluded, and more than likely going to kill me. The anger almost steams from him in physical form. The beast that stole so much from me well over a year ago is back to take what little remains of my soul.

"Why did you attack me?" I ask, anxious for answers and to keep him talking.

"You were just a job. Don't think you're special, Nina. You're just one of many."

"A job? I don't understand."

"Of course you don't, because you're too blind to see. You lived next door to a pervert who used to hire whores who looked like you to suck his dick. The night I came for you I caught him on your porch, rubbing one out while he sniffed the sun lounger where your sweet little pussy would sweat your scent in to the cushion. He thought with the storm brewing so heavily you wouldn't hear him out there, and you didn't because you were too busy trying to keep your insides from falling out of your pussy." He laughs. "How was the damage by the way?"

He paces the floor, taking too much pleasure in his cruelty, and I stare in confusion. "Mr. Ilavich went away.

He wasn't even there then."

"He lied. He wanted to get you in his house, so he told you some shit about feeding the dog, when all he wanted to do was force feed you his dick. He saw my face so he had to die." He shrugs casually, as though killing someone was as daily a chore as fetching in the morning paper.

"How did you kill him?" I need to know. He was killed because of me. Pervert or not, did that make him deserving of a death sentence?

He licks his lips and rubs his hands together. "Painfully, fortunately. I was quite inventive with him. I tossed him and his dog down the basement stairs, broke both his legs. Of course, I had to cut out the loud prick's tongue so he couldn't scream for help. Very loud, your neighbor, wasn't he? I locked the door and waited for the yappy little fucker to get hungry. It took three days before he turned on Mr. Ilavich. Teddy loved his master's meat very much." He laughs at his own joke.

Vomit claws up my chest and burns the back of my throat. "You're a monster."

"You're right, but I'm a hired one."

A gasp escapes my lips.

"You really don't see how jealous she is of you, do you?"

"Who?" I scream, sick of his games. Doesn't he see the damage he has already done? I'm broken. I'll never recover from this.

"Tricia! That dirty slut was so bitter about you. You remind her of her mother, you knew that, right? God, the amount of times I had to gag her to stop her ranting about how perfect you are and how her boyfriend wanted to fuck you, and how Todd wanted to date you. She hated how perfect you are to everyone."

"You're lying!" I get to my feet, grab a cup from the table, and launch it at him. "You're lying!" The cup crashes against his head, causing him to stumble to the side, and blood wells, dripping from the abrasion it's caused. "She wouldn't do that, that's insane! She's my best friend!"

He blinks at me, stepping back as if stunned. His chest heaves and he shakes his head. "She's dead, Nina. I killed her for what she did to you." His voice is softer and thick with emotion. It's like he's transformed before I can even blink.

"What?" I whisper, the disarray in my head making my heart beat quicker as I try to keep up with him.

He turns to face me with tears brimming in his eyes. "I didn't know. He wouldn't tell me who hired us, Nina. I didn't . . ."

"Devon, what is going on? Who is the he you're referring to? I don't understand." He tries to come closer but I hold my hand out, stopping him as my body trembles with fear. "Please, don't. Please, please, please. No more."

"I don't know what's happening . . . what I've done. Who am I, Nina?"

"You're a monster, Devon. You've destroyed me."

He grabs me before I can get away, throwing his arms around me and pulling me so tight that it physically burns my skin. "Say my name, Nina. Tell me who you love. Tell me you love me. Please keep me here, Nina. Don't let him take me, take you."

I can't breathe as tears clog my eyes and throat. Fear and confusion hold me hostage. Everything is too much and I can feel my mind leaving my body.

"I can smell the fear on you. You hum of it, and it only fuels the animal inside me, Nina." As if someone clicked their fingers, Devon has transformed yet again, the evilness inside him once again coming to the forefront. His arms are still around me, holding me in place, and his words thrash out like a razor-tipped whip. "I'm going to fuck you within an inch of your life, pull all the insides out for Devon to photograph. He's my brother, my baby brother. We've always been there for each other. We only have each other. You can't always fight the creature that lives under the surface. Devon can let his lay dormant for a while but the subconscious beast always rises to take its rightful place. When you're gone, he will see his true nature and embrace what he truly is."

Urine runs down my legs, the wet warmth of it shaming me, but I'm petrified of how he plans to kill me. Because I know he *will* kill me. This is what he promised a year ago.

"And what is he?" I ask on a choked sob.

"A refection of me."

Gravel crunches outside the window from a car skidding onto my drive and both Devon and I look towards the sound in bewilderment. Devon's hand grips my throat and he drags me over to the knife block on the counter in the kitchen, my feet digging into the floor as I try to break free from his fierce hold. Pulling out the carving knife, he forces me to move to the window, and as I'm about to scream, he plunges the knife into my leg and then pulls it out. I collapse to the floor with my hands pressing over the oozing wound. The agony is immense, the depth of it so intense that I can't even scream out.

"Stay there," he hisses.

Forty-Four

Luke

There's something not right about Devon Trent. My senses were on high alert the moment I met him. Although I can see why Nina would go for someone like him, his looks and his smile out of a magazine, I noticed the subtle glint in his eyes and the way he watched me when he didn't think I was looking. His short temper is troubling, his anger materializing in a split second, and his paranoia scared me. The way he accused Nina so easily wasn't good, or the way he had jumped down my throat when I'd asked him the simple question of where he came from. Why would he be that way unless he had something to hide?

The graphic images of the two murder victims up at Point Rose Lake keep plaguing me and I can't help the suspicion gnawing at me; it's all too coincidental. Devon moves in next door to Nina, who is the survivor of a brutal assault where there are no known suspects and her attacker is still at large, and then there are two horrific murders in town, the first in almost four decades.

I checked the lease on Mr. Brochovich's home to try and find any details about Devon, but I'd found it wasn't registered to him. Everything was in the name Mr. Devon Noah. And lo and behold, there was no Devon Noah in the system.

When I visited him at his home I only had one thing in mind; get a fingerprint. I knew he wouldn't give it to me willingly so I asked for a glass of water and then distracted him while using a strip of scotch tape already in my pocket ready for the opportunity. Life got pretty hectic around here and I'm only now getting Brady working on it and trying to get a match, or find anything on Devon to give us a clue about who he is.

"Luke, I entered the print and came up with nothing, so I ran both Devon Noah and Devon Trent and came up with a few hits, but this one stood out because there's a Noah Trent mentioned as well." Brady drops the printout on my desk. It's from a Detroit local newspaper report.

Family perishes in deadly fire:
Firefighters battled a house fire into the early hours of the morning at a house in the Redgrove area of Detroit.

County Sheriff spokesmen, Robert Allan said, "Forty-eight-year-old Joseph Trent, along with his wife, thirty-six-year-old Trudy Trent, stepdaughter Courtney Vallis, 15, and Son Noah Trent, 20, all perished in the blaze. Neighbors came to help but were pushed back by the rising flames and toxic smoke. According to onlookers, the youngest son, Devon Trent, watched in horror while his family home burned at a rapid rate. Devon then left the scene, running, and has yet to be located.

The cause of the fire has yet to be established but we can confirm we are looking at suspected arson and an investigation is underway. The ongoing search is now in place for Devon Trent. Any information please contact 080 -3331 -101

"I also got a hit with Devon registering with Dr. Hammond, but nothing after the fire article or before he came here," Brady adds but then lifts a brow at me. "We also have a hit on the small blood sample found a few meters from where the bodies were found at the lake. You ready for this?"

"Just tell me," I demand, already putting on my jacket to go see Dr. Hammond.

"The sample matches one taken from a brutal rape at a home in Kansas. The victim . . ."

"Nina Drake," I breathe, finishing his sentence.

"Yeah. How did you know that?"

I rush past him, shouting for him to follow me.

The drive takes seven minutes, and in those minutes Brady hasn't shut up about all the horrible things that pig did to Nina. I hate that he read her file. She'd be mortified if she knew. It physically hurts me knowing what she went through, and how incredible she is to have survived and keep on surviving every day since.

"They had to remove her womb, the damage was so intense." He shakes his head in disgust.

I want to be wrong about Devon. Despite the growing fondness I have for Nina, I'll gladly keep it to myself, buried under the rubble of shit I can't control and watch her be happy from afar so long as she's happy and safe. But the clawing instincts inside me tell me I'm not wrong. They see something lurking in Devon's eyes, a darkness seen only in men lacking souls.

"Sheriff Logan." Dr. Hammond smiles warmly in welcome. "Not a health call, I hope?"

I smile at the doctor who saw me through my very accident-prone adolescence and shake my head. "I actually need to ask you if you took any blood from a Devon Trent."

Her brow raises and she looks to her receptionist, whose eyes widen a little. "Come into my office, Luke."

I follow her inside. She goes straight to her filing cabinet. "I was just telling Lori, my receptionist, she's way behind uploading the blood work to the patient files and how important is it to have them on record. The lab still has the sample. I can call them for you if you like, and release the blood work?"

"That would great, thank you."

I radio through to Gerry at the office and tell him to get in touch with the lab to cross reference the blood samples found at the murder scene with the one the surgery sent in.

Brady's voice comes over the radio. "Logan, I'm coming in. I have something."

"Copy that," I reply, and offer an apologetic smile at Dr. Hammond.

"The information has just been uploaded but here are the files in case you need them. Is there something wrong with Mr. Trent? He appeared troubled, I must admit." She hands me his file.

Brady rushes through the door without knocking. "The partial print just flagged up on the system, a match. It's him, Luke, that Devon guy. Nina's boyfriend is the same person who killed them, who raped her."

A gasp sounds out into the room from Dr. Hammond and I want to chastise him for being so careless with information in front of civilians, but I understand his shock and outburst. My insides are coiling and preparing myself for what's to come.

"Slow down. Tell me what happened."

"The system in the office is running slow and it took a while to connect the prints. The one from Devon that I uploaded today matches the partial taken from the dead girl's locket at Point Rose Lake." He's out of breath, the urgent look in his eyes matching my own.

"I need you to go back to the station, arm yourself, and call in everyone available then meet me at Devon's house."

"You can't go there alone, Luke!"

"Brady, just do what I tell you. I need to go get Nina."

Forty-Five

Nina

MY BLOOD IS PUMPING FAST from the wound but the pain is overruled by the fear of him hurting Luke. "Devon's crazy and he has a knife!" I scream out in hope to warn him from coming in without precaution.

"You'll pay for that betrayal, Nina."

Everything happens so quickly, the terror raging my body and the loss of blood making everything blurry and unrefined, like I'm watching a movie play out at the cinema. The tip of a gun comes through the side door, both of Luke's hands wrapped around it firmly as his body comes in to view. His eyes are everywhere as he searches his surroundings, then when he sees me they widen and he rushes forwards.

I shake my head frantically, the only vocal warning I can manage is a whimper as I try and prevent him from letting his guard down, but it's too late. The need to come to me overrules everything he's been taught and before a warning scream can rip from my chest, Devon grabs Luke's arm, causing the gun to drop and skid across the floor. I watch in horror when, with quick jabs to Luke's abdomen before he can even react, Devon stabs him multiple times then steps away from him. Bewilderment furrows Luke's brow, clouded confusion in his eyes as he looks down at his stomach and watches the beige cotton of his shirt spread out with dots of crimson soaking through, staining everywhere. His legs buckle and he looks over at me with so much sorrow. "I'm sorry," he breathes.

I cry out, my scream a choked sob of panic when I can do nothing but watch the extent of Devon's evil unfold before me. I cry and try to crawl over to Luke, my own wound hindering my need to help my friend. He's a good man. He's going to die because of me, because I was too blind to see the immorality living inside Devon.

"Aww, how nice. The Sheriff's sweet on my brother's girl." Devon sneers, the ice in his eyes freezing my soul when he mocks me. "He can watch me dismantle you before he bleeds out."

His footsteps pound the floor towards me, each vibration ricocheting through my heart as I try to scramble away. He grabs my ankles and yanks me across the floor until I'm only a couple of feet from Luke, whose hand leaves his bleeding stomach to reach out for me. The blood from his hand drips across the floor, each drop thundering in my ears like an earthquake. My jeans are ripped from my body and all I can do is focus on Luke's eyes as a tear runs down the side of his nose. He growls when my panties are cut from me, the knife digging into the flesh and leaving a deep burning cut.

"Your cunt looks a lot prettier then I left it, Nina. Let's see how inventive I can be this time."

Luke's eyes lift, followed by his eyebrows, and I track their stare to his gun. I inhale a breath and reach for it. Pain slices through my palm and I cry out in both agony and hopelessness when Devon's knife impales my hand and pins me to the floor, the deep hue of my blood mixing with Luke's when it spreads like a river across the light-wood floor.

Devon laughs coldly, his delight merciless and punishing as his eyes dance with manic excitement. But it's short lived when a fist collides with the side of his face and the sound pitching from Luke as he digs deep for enough strength to make a second blow is heart wrenching.

I take the chance to reach up with my other hand and grab the gun, my body twisting abnormally as strength and determination drives me. A cry of relief leaves me as the heavy metal handle graces my palm. I rotate my body and aim the gun right at the forehead of the man I love. He's leaning over me with mystification written all over his features. His eyes are unfocused and searching, his mouth open and his brow pinched tightly together.

"What's happening?" he pleads, and I know it's Devon looking down at me, his love for me once more strong and full.

He looks down my body, his eyes widening on my naked and bleeding legs. Confusion morphs his handsome face before realization sinks in and the look of horror and self-abhorrence makes me want to cry out. Then he looks across at Luke dying. Tears spring in his eyes and he releases a distraught scream, every ache he ever felt, every rejection he ever faced and every false memory bursting from him in the most torturous cry. He knows. He understands finally.

Gently, his hands cup around mine and he holds them there with the gun at his head. My tears are as fluid as his, both our hearts breaking as one when he whispers, "I love you, Nina. Believe me, believe that I always loved you, since the day I first saw you. Don't let me take your beauty, or your soul."

He smiles so softly as his finger slips over mine and he squeezes.

Epilogue; Forty-Six

Nina

Three months later

"Hey." Heather smiles at me as she walks through the door. There are tears in her eyes. This is the first time we have ever been physically face to face.

I stand from the couch in her waiting room. "Hi."

For some reason, we're both emotional and my tears are as fluid as hers as we embrace, for the first time able to touch and smell each other.

"Goodness me." She laughs as she whips us both a tissue from the box on her receptionist's desk. "Come on in."

She grins at me.

It seems strange looking around her room in real life instead of through a laptop screen. She gestures to one of the comfy armchairs and I sit. "Tea, coffee or water? Although I feel like we should be drinking champagne."

I laugh and nod. "Coffee is fine." It feels like I'm having a catch up and coffee with a girlfriend and I'm surprised by how relaxed I already am in Heather's presence, but then again, we have been talking every week for eighteen months. It's no wonder we're close. She knows things about me that no one ever knew before.

Placing our drinks on the small table between us, she settles back into her own chair and smiles at me. "You're looking good."

I grin and nod, taking a large breath. "I am. I am good." I never thought I would utter those words again, yet here I am.

"Is it over?"

I ponder Heather's question. I know she means personally, in my head, and finally, I nod. "It's over."

Tipping her head, she regards me when a tear leaks from my eyes. "What's upsetting you?"

I pick up my drink and take a sip. She even knows how much cream and sugar I take without having to ask me. I'm sure it was covered in one of our casual conversations somewhere. "I can't help but feel stupid."

"Why stupid?"

"Well, come on. I fell in love with the very man that brutalized me for four very long hours. How could I not tell?"

She nods, sipping her own drink. "I think that's understandable, Nina. However, how much do you actually know about Dissociative Identity Disorder?"

"A lot more than I used to," I answer wryly.

"Yes, I would imagine." She shifts from her seat and approaches her desk, slipping out some printed sheets before handing them to me. "I took the liberty of getting some information on the subject for you."

I take the sheets from her but sigh. "What I don't get is, his voice, his eyes..."

"Nina," Heather says quietly as she reaches over and takes my hand. "In most cases, those with DID, their alter egos are completely different people. Some take on a completely different accent, some even speak in a foreign tongue. Devon and Noah were, if you like, two completely different men."

"Like Jekyll and Hyde?"

"Exactly like that. Devon will have had no memory of Noah's interactions, and vice versa." She sighs and leans back again. "It is thought that a trauma in childhood triggers the onset. And in Devon's case, the death of his whole family, at his hands, would have most likely been the trigger. It was his only way of coping. His brother, Noah, no matter how evil a person, was still his brother, and Devon felt bonded to him. So his mind gave him Noah, albeit out of himself, but to Devon he was very real, alive and most definitely a separate entity to him."

She senses my dilemma and smiles at me as she reaches forwards again. "Nina, it's okay to love him."

I nod. She'd hit the nail on the head. "It sickens me. Yet I can't help this ache inside me. I hate that I miss him, that I'm grieving for him."

"It's good that you're grieving for him. You need to. It was Noah who assaulted you, Noah who broke you and I would imagine, Noah who broke Devon in the end. But you have to remember that Devon loved you. Yes, his life was full of atrocious acts but then, with what I've learned about his childhood, who would have come out of that mentally unscathed? I'm not condoning what he, or rather, they did, but when you've been in my line of business for so long, you get to realize that no one is 'normal'. Normal isn't even a word I would ever use because we're all different, in every way."

My mouth dries and I sigh. "Luke thinks I'm crazy that I want to visit his grave."

"It doesn't matter what Luke or anyone else thinks, Nina. You need to do what is best for you, and if visiting Devon's grave, once or every day, is what you need to help you move on then that's what you do. It is your life and you're the only one who can find a way of moving on."

"I'm still finding it hard to trust. I'm not sure what to think about Tricia and the fact she's gone and I can never get to the truth."

"And that is something we will continue to work on. Getting you to a place where you can accept the things out of your control. We don't always know why people do the things they do, I'm afraid. Life would be a lot simpler if we did."

Placing my empty cup on the table, I stand up. She stands with me and walks out into the reception area where Luke is waiting for me. He quickly gets up from the couch. "Okay?"

"I'm glad you're up and about Sheriff Logan."

He shakes his head and offers his hand. "Please, you can call me Luke. And I have a few scars but I survived." He looks over at me with a glaze in his eyes and takes my hand in his. "We survived."

Heather smiles as she looks down at our hands and I giggle lightly at the proud glint in her eyes.

"So, we good?" he asks.

I look up to him and smile. "Yeah." I nod, "Yeah, I think we will be."

He gives me that smile that's only reserved for me and nods. "Then let's go home."

"Home," I whisper to myself with a smile. A smile that hasn't graced my face for two years. A real one, a smile full of hope and optimism. Because after everything, I'm a stronger person, a woman who can now cope with whatever life throws at me. And by God, if I'm not eager for it.

Devon has, in some ways, taught me the most important lesson of all. Grab what life gives you and cherish it because we never knew when it will be whipped from under us. In his case, it had been his family. And as I look slyly at Luke gazing softly at me, I know that it's my turn for a family. A family that will finally love me for exactly who I am. A strong and tough woman.

Nina Francis Drake.

The End

Coming Soon

Night Fires

By D H Sidebottom

I would watch him watch the ocean. He would build fires and sit, all night waiting.

For her. For his dead wife.

She never came. I never expected her to. But he did. And he never let go.

Even when I fell in love with him he never let go.

Until the night of the storm. The night my worst nightmares came to life.

And I lost everything to her when she finally returned.

For us both.

Coming Soon

TEN
(A Brother's ~~best~~ friend romance)

By Ker Dukey

Alexandria (alex)

My brother Jonah was possessive when it came to the things he owned; this unfortunately included the people in his life. The forbidden love between his best friend and me was just that . . . forbidden.

Our families were from different walks of life and as a sheriff's daughter being with a Moore's kid would never be tolerated. To my parents their son and Dalton Moore were on different paths and their friendship would end as soon as college began but it was my brother who had a craving for trouble. He was always looking for danger, committing petty crimes and getting away with it because Dalton would take the fall, blackening his already stained name. When Jonah found out we broke the rules by loving each other, his consequences impacted us all with immeasurable suffering.

Betrayal comes with a debt and it would be paid by all of us.

> One with their heart,
> one with their mind
> and one would pay in blood.

Acknowledgements

Thank you to everyone who made this title possible. Our wonderful betas

Our amazing 'Kinky Kittens' street team, who work so hard and selflessly promoting us.

Stacey our incredible formatter and Kyra our awesome editor